ZODIAC SAGA 2

The Balance of Power

Kaitlyn McKnight

ZODIAC SAGA 2

McKnight Publishing Group
PO Box 10465 Gulfport MS 39505

ISBN 978-0-9894894-4-7

Printed in the United States of America

For everyone who bought the first book, for everyone who has been told "no", for everyone who is odd, strange, or a little eccentric, this is for you.

Origin of the Story

A bullied 12-year-old young boy named Cyrus O'Hara, who is now 13-years-old and known as Lancaster, believed in Zodiac gods. He proved the existence of the Zodiac gods by finding the Temple of Zodia where they dwelled. The Zodiac gods are also known as the Sacred Twelve or The Elders of Zodia. One of the Zodiac gods had a vison of a malevolent entity that would destroy the world. Now an unknown powerful force is seeking to destroy the Zodiac gods and the entire universe. Lancaster embarks upon a suspenseful journey with friends Sofia the fearless, Peter the great, and Judas the ghoul to save the world. Along the way they will encounter new friends, old friends, new foes, and old foes. A tragic turn of events leads Lancaster on a path to reveal a hidden secret about the Sacred Twelve. This secret helps him learn more about the meaning of family and his own true identity.

Table of Contents

The Unexpected

With Cancer as our pilot, we wandered the big blue sky endlessly. It took three months to get to Seattle Washington. Cancer, the pilot, made multiple stops and layovers exploring different cities. We thank him for his help, but we still didn't like him completely. Afterall it is his fatal error in the temple that caused the gems to be lost. I had a really bad feeling about him. We were granted permission to land at an airport. The friendly airport security men escorted us into the terminal. We were able to get a map of Seattle and rent a car. Peter started the blue Corolla and pulled away from the airport parking lot.

It was dead silence until Sofia sighed. "I can't believe this is actually happening."

I smiled from the backseat. "You mean helping the Elders?"

She looked back at me and frowned. "No. I'm talking about traveling the world. That's the only reason why I want to help the Elders." Sofia did a faint smile. She had started wearing glasses and of course they were purple.

Judas did a silent ghoulish laugh. "I'm only doing this because I have one of their Gems." Judas got his hair cut in a military style. He had dyed his hair the same color as Sofia's highlights. He said it was because he didn't want to wear hats anymore. His skin wasn't quite as pale but he still looked ghoulish.

Peter stayed quiet. He never liked to talk when he was driving. He wasn't the world's best driver so he would always ignore things going on around him. He'd grown his hair out longer so it overlapped on his ears. He stopped wearing his sun glasses for some unknown reason. He traded his muscle shirts for regular T-shirts. He didn't smile as often as he used to.

I sat back. "I'm not in it for the adventure or because I have one of their Gems. I'm in it…"

"Because of your dad, right?" Judas asked interrupting me. "Or is it because you want the Elders to be kind to you?"

"Neither. I want to do this because I don't want the world to be destroyed again."

Through the pull-down visor mirror, I could see Sofia roll her eyes.

Judas hit my shoulder. "You're to honest, Lancaster."

"So, you guys are kidding?"

Judas sighed. "Take a nap."

Judas was the one who ended up taking a nap. Sofia took pictures as we passed by different places. Peter kept his eyes on the road. I was sitting back playing with the metal ball my dad gave me. I would morph it into a small ballerina then into a tiger then into a monkey eating a banana. I kept making shapes and objects until Peter slammed on brakes causing Judas's drool to whack me in my eye. The sudden stop made Sofia drop her camera and caused her to violently curse twice. As for Judas, he woke up seeing his mouth drool drip off of my face.

"Sorry." Judas said trying to wipe the saliva off with his jacket sleeve.

Sofia scoffed at Peter. "Peter, why the heck did you slam on brakes like that?!" She picked up her camera and tried to turn it on. "It's broken!"

I got out of my seatbelt and took the camera from her. "Give me a minute or two."

She folded her arms. "I'm waiting for an answer, Peter."

He sighed. "It… it was nothing."

Judas shook his head. "One thing I have learned is that whenever somebody says it was nothing that means it is something."

"We know, Judas." Sofia said in an agitated voice. "Answer truthfully, O'Hara." She said to Peter.

I was still sitting back trying to use Aquarius to fix Sofia's camera, but I still commented saying. "Maybe Peter saw something in the road and tried not to hit it."

Judas put his hand on my shoulder saying. "Or maybe there's another explanation. Peter?"

Peter sighed again. "It really doesn't matter. Let's just find a hotel."

Sofia ran her tongue across her teeth then looked forward and sat back. "Just drive Peter O'Hara."

Peter very slowly pulled back onto the road.

Judas sat back and looked at me. "Don't worry; I won't go to sleep again."

I smiled. "Thanks." I kept trying to fix the camera. There were scratches and dints all over it.

Peter stopped again only slower this time. He looked in the rearview mirror and smiled. "It's a red light."

I laughed to myself. Thankfully this time Sofia didn't curse. I sat back then realized that I didn't put my seatbelt back on. I went to reach for it, but something terrible happened. A car slammed into us.

I was sent flying passed Peter then through the windshield. I could feel the glass jab into my skin. I landed on the ground. My vision went blurry. All I could see was a haze of blood and glass. Then I saw Sofia's camera. Metal pieces were scattered everywhere. I did a painful sigh. I would soon meet Aries again. I opened my eyes thinking that I would see the broken dark road and then my secret uncle would come and greet me as he did before. Everything would be the same except more people would be there and I wouldn't be able to return to earth. That's what I thought. What actually happened was not what I expected.

When my eyes opened, I saw Mercy hovering over me. She was covered in blood. She sighed in discussed. "Finally, you decide to wake up."

I sat up and looked around. I was in the middle of the road. "Where is everybody… did they die?"

The corner of her mouth lifted then quickly went back down. "They're fine. They're at the hospital."

I tried to sit up but I couldn't so I lay back down on the bumpy road. "Why aren't I at the hospital?"

She stood up. I could now see her yellow skinny jeans and orange tank top. They were bloodstained. "Your friends thought you were dead so they were going to put you in a body bag. Luckily I came and convinced them to leave you here for now and so they went on to the hospital."

She licked her lips. "I used magic to save you."

"If you used magic why are you covered in my blood?

Looking irritated she rolled her eyes. "Would you rather be dead?"

"Yes, maybe, I mean no."

She helped me to my feet. "Come on let's go see your friends."

"Wait." I said. "Do you know who hit us?"

She looked back at me. "No."

"How did you know that we got into a car wreck?"

She signed in annoyance. "It was all on the news. Come on."

I tried to walk but I fell down hard. "Help." I said reaching up toward her.

She looked at me and I actually saw worry in her eyes. She quickly reached down and helped me up. I put my arm around her neck and we started walking to her car. I remembered the first time I rode in her car. She gave me answers to all of my questions. Now I hope she will answer questions for me again.

She opened the passenger door. "Try not to get blood on the seat."

I frowned. "Really? Just use your magic to change my clothes into something less bloody and torn by glass."

She patted my back. "Why waste my magic?"

"So, you want your car to be bloody? Okay am fine with that."

"Get in." She lightly shoved me into the car. I buckled my seatbelt then looked through the visor mirror. I saw Patrick, her magical green cat sitting in the backseat, just like before. He jumped to the front seat and curled up in my lap.

I looked over at Mercy who already had her seatbelt on and was ready to drive. "I thought Patrick was dead." I said pointing to the cat.

"Magic is real." She said cranking up the car. She drove off just like before, fast.

"Mercy, I just got into a car accident so please slow down."

She didn't take her eyes off the road. "Lancaster, your friends are in critical condition and you want me to slow down?"

"Yes, I want you to slow down. I would like to at least arrive alive to the hospital."

She rolled her eyes and sighed while ignoring what I said.

"So, is rolling your eyes and sighing your signature trademark?"

She reached over and hit me. "Shut up." She sped up even faster.

I ran my hand up and down Patrick's back then whispered in his ear, "Nice to see you again, Patrick." He purred softly.

Out of the corner of my eye I could see Mercy smile and nod. "Why are you so nice?"

"Because being nice is a good thing."

She started to sigh but stopped herself. "A good thing. Wow. Aren't you just like your father."

"Am I really?" I said excitedly.

She went to roll her eyes but quickly looked down instead. "Just stop talking."

The drive to the hospital was an hour with Mercy driving fast. If anyone else were driving I would assume that it would have taken longer. Mercy parked in a designated handicap park and I thought to myself, really. Then she finally used her magic to clean up our bloody torn clothes. We exited the car then entered the ER section of the hospital.

The young woman at the front desk looked to be in her twenties. She was on the phone having a serious conversation. By serious I mean they were talking about her new boots.

Mercy waved her hands to get the woman's attention. "Excuse me; we are looking for some patients…"

The woman cut her off. She took her phone away from her ear. "Yeah that's great don't care. If you want to find whoever, look at this thing." She slid a clipboard to us then resumed her conversation.

While Mercy was trying to find the room numbers, I was staring around the waiting area. It was half vacant. Only five people were in the little area. All were busy watching the news. It was talking about some major car accident that happened two and a half hours ago......... OH! I sat in one of the chairs and started to listen also.

"The accident took no prisoners." The anchorwoman said. "As you can see behind me, this was a tragic accident. One of the people has been reported dead. The others are in critical condition in the hospital. This accident was indeed tragic and the other vehicle fled the scene. I completely understand why. The police are still looking for the other car. If you have any information about this car wreck, please contact the police immediately." She went off the screen.

So basically Peter, Judas, and Sofia are in critical condition. On the other hand, I'm dead... wow... just wow.

Mercy put her hand on my shoulder. "I found their rooms."

I stood up. "Good."

We walked to the door that led to the ER rooms. I tried to open the door but it was locked. In order to enter you had to have some type of special card to scan on the door scanner.

Mercy pushed me back. "This is where magic comes in." She set her finger on the scanner and it made a beeping noise. She turned to me. "Be a gentleman and open the door."

I opened the door and she stepped in first. I followed closely behind her. We walked around the place for ten minutes. Finally, Mercy stopped walking.

"Okay," she started, "Peter is in the room directly down the hall on the left. Sofia is in the room across from Peter's."

"What about Judas?" I asked.

She sighed quietly. "He wasn't on the list."

"But the news said that everyone but me survived."

"I'm not saying that he's dead, all I'm saying is that he wasn't on the list."

I grunted. "I'll go to Peter's room; you go to Sofia's."

7

I started to walk down the hall but she stopped me. "Uh, no. You go to Sofia's room and I'll go to Peter's."

"Why?" I asked.

"Because, I don't like her." She turned around and started walking down the hall. She opened a door then stepped inside out of sight. The door shut with a loud echo.

When I got to Sofia's room, I expected to see her lying on the bed in pain. Instead, she was sitting up in one of the chairs. She didn't notice me until I shut the door.

She jumped up from her seat. "Lancaster… I thought you were dead… or are we both dead?"

I sat in the chair next to hers. "We're both alive. Mercy used magic to save me."

She sat back down. "Mercy saved you?"

"Yeah."

She shifted uncomfortably in her chair. "Where is she now?"

"That doesn't matter right now. How are you feeling, are you okay? The news said…"

She held up her hand. "Let me stop you there. Don't always believe what the news says. Anyway, I'm okay because…" She did a long pause. "…Because my daddy watches over me."

"Daddy?"

"Taurus."

"Oh, right. Well what about Peter?"

She shrugged her shoulders. "I haven't seen him yet."

"What about Judas?"

"I haven't seen him yet either."

"Mercy said that he wasn't on the hospital list."

She shook her head. "Judas can't die because he's already dead."

"So, where is he?"

"I don't know."

"You want to go check on Peter then?"

She stood up. "Yes, sure."

We walked across the hall to one of the other doors. I opened the door and we saw Mercy sitting in the chair beside the bed Peter was in.

Peter's eyes were closed and his heart rate was getting slower and slower. I walked over to Mercy. "Save him."

She looked at me. "I can't."

Sofia pushed her way pass me. "Why not, Mercy?"

Mercy stood up. "Because I'm… grounded. I'm not supposed to use magic."

"But you used magic on me and saved my life." I reminded her.

"Yeah, but I wasn't supposed to. Virgo somehow found out and now I'm in bigger trouble." She said.

Sofia walked closer to Mercy. "Since when do you care about what your mother says?"

Mercy folded her arms. "Shut up. At least I don't always have to fall back on my dad."

Sofia folded her arms. "At least I have a dad."

"Okay both of you stop." I said walking in between them. "Just save Peter, please."

"I can't." Mercy yelled.

Sofia pushed me to the ground to move closer to Mercy again. "You can but you won't." She said to her.

"Why don't you ask your daddy what to say next?" Mercy yelled to Sofia.

"Why don't you ask your sister what to do after I'm done kicking your butt?" Sofia yelled to Mercy.

As the two argued and yelled I started to remember something. I remembered what Mercy told me before. Sofia's mom killed Mercy's sister so Virgo killed Sofia's mom. That comment Sofia made had to hit one of Mercy's nerves. Mercy's hands and eyes glowed blue. Two silhouettes came from Sofia. One covered the front of her the other covered the back of her. Her purple eyes glowed. Mercy then made her entire body glow blue.

"This time, I'll kill you." Mercy said to Sofia.

Sofia's eyes flickered as she talked. "Try it."

I stood back up and got in between them again. "Please don't fight."

They both looked at me and said nothing. I backed up. "Okay fine by me, go ahead and fight it out. May the strongest girl win and whatever."

They both charged simultaneously. Sofia had defense, but Mercy had offense. Mercy was able to push Sofia through the wall. Mercy looked at me and smiled. Then she ran off to kill Sofia.

I looked at Peter's heart rate. It was even slower now. I sighed and kneeled at his bedside. "What do I do now?" We didn't even start our journey yet and already bad things were happening. Then suddenly I heard people screaming and a lot of glass breaking. "Great." I ran out the room to try to find a doctor.

Three hallways down I found a nerdy doctor sitting in a corner. He was in a feeble position and crying. Broken glass was all around him. He looked up and saw me then ran to me. "What is going on here?!"

I took his arm and started running for the room Peter was in. "Doctor my bro, I mean my friend is dying and I need your help."

When we made it to the room, Peter was sitting up at the edge of the bed laughing. I let go of the doctor's arm and walked slowly over to Peter. "Peter?"

He jumped down. "What?"

"How are you doing, are you okay?" I stepped back an inch.

He patted my head and smiled. "Let's just get going."

"But how are you feeling?!" I asked again.

He looked out into the hallway. There was destruction everywhere the eye can see. "What happened here? What is going on, did Armageddon come or something?"

"No, Sofia and Mercy are battling it out. I tried to stop them but you know, it was a lost cause."

He put his hand on my shoulder and started walking with me. I told him "don't worry, their parents will stop them. Now, what about Judas?"

"Do you know where he is?"

"No" He said and scratched his face and sighed. "Let's get out of this place. I have a feeling that in a few minutes this place will be nothing but a pile of rubble."

We made our way passed every flaming wall and gaping cracked marble floor. The air smelled like smoke and caused me to occasionally cough. Every window was broken except for one. The only reason why that one window wasn't broken was because Judas was sitting down in front of it admiring the view. The view was of a large willow tree gently swaying in the air.

Peter got my attention and shook his head. "Leave him, he seems content."

We continued our path to the exit. When we made it to the exit it was sealed shut. It was sealed off by… Mercy and Sofia… right then I started to complain as they continue to fight.

"Can't we find another exit?" I asked Peter.

"No, wait." He walked over to them and smiled. "Mercy-Sofia, Girls, it's time to stop fighting."

I realized that Sofia and Mercy were now wearing gladiator armor. Mercy's armor was bronze, but Sofia's was pink. They each had matching blue hilts and glowing purple blades. They both looked at Peter and ignored him.

Peter shook his head. "You both know that your parents are going to kill you so just stop fighting now."

Mercy did her signature sigh and eye roll. "I won't stop until she's dead."

Sofia nodded. "Likewise."

They both simultaneously charged. Sofia tried to slice at Mercy's right side, but Mercy cleverly parried to the ground. She came up slowly slicing at Sofia. Sofia stepped back and lost her balance. Mercy found that to be the perfect opportunity. She cut at Sofia's right side. The sword cut through the armor and caused Sofia to yell. Mercy drew first blood. Sofia clumsily stood to her feet with her free hand at her side.

Mercy laughed. "Give up?"

Sofia tried her best to smile. "I don't give up." She tried to stab at her opponent's stomach, but she parried once again.

The sorceress Mercy cleverly twirled her sword to intimidate her wounded opponent Sofia. Mercy motioned as if she was going to cut at Sofia's stomach but in actuality she cut at her throat. Sofia blocked her stomach but then quickly realized that she was tricked. She didn't realize it quickly enough. Her throat was cut and she fell. Her sword slid away from her.

I know what you're probably thinking. You're probably thinking why I didn't go and help Sofia. I honestly was afraid of those two killing me... okay to be even more honest sometimes I'm a wimp. I can't help that fact.

Mercy put her blade to Sofia's already bleeding throat. "You give up now?"

Sofia stayed quiet for a few moments. "Kill me."

Mercy smiled. "Last words, daddy's girl?"

Sofia closed her eyes. "May you die at the hand of your father."

Mercy raised her sword. That's when I decided to stop being a wimp... at that moment. I tried to use the Aquarius gem to stop the sword blade... only it didn't work. "What the heck."

Mercy looked over at me and shook her head saying. "This sword is made out of magic not metal, your gem will not work."

Then a light bulb turned on in my head. I tried using Aquarius to move her armor... that didn't work either.

She laughed. "My armor is also made of magic." She held out her hand and I was sent levitating in the air toward her. She stopped me when I was spitting distance away from her. "You're really starting to annoy me, Lancaster." Her hand closed and I fell. She lifted up her sword at Sofia again. Suddenly I didn't think anymore. I just started to react.

I grabbed the sword from Mercy's hands and set the blade against her neck. "Do you give up?"

She smiled. "You don't have the heart to kill anyone."

"So, you think."

Her eyes moved from side to side. "Lancaster, I can easily kill you with one word."

I gulped. "Then why don't you?"

"Because I want you to feel like the hero. I want you to believe that you saved your friend Sofia."

"Sofia!" I looked down at her. She was sitting up looking at me nearly breathless bleeding from the neck. I was tempted to drop the sword and go over to her when she collapsed. I could either save Sofia or kill Mercy now. "You save her now!" I yelled out to Mercy pressing the sword to her neck.

"No." Mercy said with pep.

I put more pressure to her neck and once more yelled. "Save her!"

Mercy then pointed her hand behind me and said "look." I slowly turned my head to look and everything changed in an instant. I dropped the sword immediately as my eyes looked around. I saw all the Elders behind me. None of them smiled except for Cancer. Not even my dad smiled at me.

Cancer waved at me. "Hi, Lancaster! Btw, you are in so much trouble."

As I turned completely around, I saw Peter standing off to the side of the Elders. He shook his head and put his hand over his mouth.

I did a fake smile. "Oh, hello.

"Allow me to enlighten you all with everything that's going on. By the looks of things here, you may be thinking that I went on a rampage through the hospital. Then decided to try and kill Sofia and then get Mercy to save her. That is what Mercy told you, right, that I was the one who injured Sofia."

"Silence" an authoritative voice said.

The Zodians were trying to determine my fate because they thought I was trying to kill Mercy and Sofia. Taurus was suggesting that he kill me with his bare finger (yes, he said finger). Leo wanted to feed me to the lions (I still believe that when he said lions, he really meant lion meaning himself). Scorpio wanted to send me to his son (in the name of Pisces I said no). Virgo was okay with the whole situation. In fact, she congratulated me. That made them all even angrier. The rest of the Elders (besides my dad-Aquarius, Sagittarius, and Cancer) voted for Scorpio's idea.

Gemini laughed. "Why not vote for Scorpio's idea? I mean the kids going there anyway."

Aquarius stood looking with his eyes like fire. He caused his metal throne to hit Gemini. By hit I mean that it was quickly blocked by one of Gemini's silhouettes.

Libra stood and quickly walked to Aquarius. "That is enough Aquarius."

Aquarius folded his arms. "I will not sit here and allow her to say such things like that about Lancaster my son."

"Then stand." Libra walked back to his throne and seated himself. "Fix your throne." He said to Aquarius.

With a simple glance Aquarius throne came back to its original place. He sat down looking at me. I gave him a secret smile and he did the same.

Gemini exhaled hard. "Now back to the real matter. This boy… this son of Aquarius tried to kill his friends. He's not as good and pure as you all thought he was."

I held up my index finger. "Hold on a second. You still haven't given me the chance to tell my side of the story."

Virgo nodded. "Let's hear it then." She crossed her legs. "Go ahead, tell us what happened at the hospital."

So, I told them everything starting from the car crash to now. I gave them every little detail possible. When I was done, I sat on the cold marble floor and shrugged my shoulders. "That's what really happened."

They all were silent. Only Gemini said something. "I vote we still burn him regardless."

I saw a huge blue vein appear on my dad's forehead. I ran over to him as fast as I could. I whispered to him, "Dad it's okay. She wants you to get mad to make it look like I inherited my 'anger issues' from you." While I was beside him my watch kept rattling.

He shook his head and whispered to me, "Go back to where you were. They are staring. I hate it when they stare."

I nodded and went back to where I was. I sat down on the ground again.

Aries took off his hood to reveal his ghoul face. "Allow me to take him instead of Scorpio's son."

Scorpio laughed. "Please! I know for a fact that you would just talk to the boy and maybe buy him a soda pop! I'm not a fool Aries! In fact, none of us are! Except for you Cancer."

Cancer wasn't even listening. He was too busy rocking out to his music. He looked at me and waved then resumed his music player.

Aries shook his head. "I will disciple him."

Taurus stomped his foot and sent an earthquake to me. It was a centimeter away from me. I backed up and looked at him. He looked at Aries. "How severely will you punish him? He nearly murdered my daughter and all you are going to do is make him stand in a corner for five minutes!" He stood and walked toward me.

I stood up fast and ran over to my dad. Aquarius sighed. I didn't know if he was sighing about Taurus trying to kill me or me running to him.

Taurus did an evil laugh. "Figures you would run to your father! Fight me like you fought my daughter insect!"

My watch was rattling again. I looked at Taurus and shook my head. "I would never hurt or fight Sofia. When she wakes up you can ask her what really happened."

"If she wakes up!" With a battle cry Taurus charged at me.

I used my watch to move my dad's throne from under him to me. I made the throne fit my body to protect me. But I felt a fist hit my gut. Then I felt my head press up against a wall. I could feel the blood running down my body.

The throne went away from me. I fell on my knees and looked up. Again, Aquarius used his throne as a weapon and struck Taurus's head. The hit did not affect him. Then Aquarius held his hand up and wrapped metal around Taurus's body. First his hands and arms, then his legs and feet. And then his waist up to his neck.

Taurus did another battle cry and the metal around his body started to creak. The other Zodians (including Cancer) watched them. Aquarius conjured up more metal and rapped each piece around Taurus until you could only see one of his eyes. His eye closed then opened quickly. His eye glowed like a star. He yelled then by the looks of it started punching the metal. Aquarius didn't back down. As each metal was punched away another would come and fill the spot. Cancer stood but was signaled by Libra to sit back down. He sat looking at Taurus and Aquarius like a child looks at a piece of mysterious food.

I stood up feeling more and more blood leaving my body. My stomach hurt so I clutched it with one hand. I tried to use my watch to move the throne but I couldn't concentrate. I saw Virgo stand. Her heels clattered against the floor as she walked to me. She set her hand on the back of my head. I fidgeted at first because it hurt. Then I felt the wound start to close up.

Virgo's pink eyes glowed as she smiled. When the wound was fully healed, she walked back to her vine throne. The others didn't even notice that she moved. I felt the back of my head. It was healed completely unlike my stomach. I stood up and saw that Taurus had put Aquarius in a headlock. I ran behind Taurus and jumped on his back. I moved his arms enough to release my dad's head from his grip. Taurus started shaking me around. I put my hands around his thick neck as he continuously jumped up and down trying to shake me off his back. Each time he would jump the entire room would shake. I got a massive headache on his third jump. Finally, after jumping eleven times, he reached back and grabbed my shoulders. Aquarius tried to tackle Taurus but that was an ultimate fail. Taurus pulled me over his shoulders and was about to throw me head first into the ground (yes in the ground).

That was when Libra stood and held up his hand. Taurus stopped and gently set me down on the ground. I hid behind my dad but he pulled my arm and made me stand beside him. Taurus went back to his throne and my dad went back to his throne. I sat down watching Libra.

Libra made a noise that sounded like a laugh. "This boy tried to kill no one. He is innocent."

"He is not!" Yelled Taurus.

Virgo looked at Libra. "I think his yelling just caused me to go deaf."

"To bad it didn't cause you to go mute." Cancer said cleverly.

"Shut up!" Virgo yelled to Cancer.

"I thought you went deaf." Cancer stuck out his tongue at Virgo.

"I said, I think I did. Learn to listen."

"Learn to respect." Said Cancer.

"Enough." Libra said as he sat down. "Now, let us discuss whether he is guilty or…"

"Guilty." Gemini said interrupting. "He's guilty. Can I leave now?"

Virgo rolled her eyes and sighed (just like her daughter Mercy, who probably got that trademark signature from her). "You are no different than your brother." The room went silent then. You could only hear whispers.

Their whispers sounded like angry wasps swarming. I sat on the ground listening to the angry wasps as their whispers got louder and louder. My sentence would be an eternity in fire just because I allegedly tried to kill a Zodians child. That was a harsh sentence. They really didn't like me. The angry wasps stopped their buzzing and all eyes turned to me. I observed all the grim faces (all faces were grim but my father's, even Cancer's face was grim). I smiled at them hoping that at least one grim face would smile back. And one did smile. It was… Virgo that smiled at me.

She smiled a genuine smile so that made me smile more. She looked down and a rose appeared in my hand. The other Zodians jumped and looked at her. She was still smiling and her smile was brighter than the sun. I smelled the red rose. It smelled just like a freshly picked strawberry. The dew (laugh) on the rose dripped on my hand. I looked up and saw that she was still smiling with her head down. The Elders looked at her in amazement. Aquarius was so amazed until he stood up wide-eyed looking at her.

Still smiling she lifted up her head and walked slowly to me. I smelled the strawberry scented rose again then stood up. She put her hand on my shoulder and whispered, "Fear."

She looked at the Elders and her smile faded an inch. She put her arm around me and ran her other hand through my hair. "I vote that he is innocent."

Libra nodded. "Those who agree say I, those opposed say nay."

I heard Aquarius, Aries, Libra, Cancer, Capricorn, Sagittarius, and Pisces say I. All the others I guess said nay. So, Taurus, Gemini, Leo, and Scorpio must have said nay. Taurus's voice boomed the loudest nay.

Libra nodded. "Lancaster son of Aquarius, you are innocent."

I jumped up and yelled, "Yes!" I threw both of my hands in the air. "I'm free!" I jumped in circles yelling, "I don't have to burn for an eternity!"

I stopped when Virgo put her hand on my shoulder and whispered, "That's enough. The ones that said nay are already mad."

I stopped and looked. The nays had their arms crossed and had dirty looks on their faces. I cleared my throat and bowed. "I have to go now." I turned to walk away.

"Stop." Libra instructed me. The word echoed in the room.

I turned back around. "Yes?"

He stood from his throne. "Never has Virgo used her sorcery."

"She usually uses her looks." Cancer said laughing.

Both Libra and Virgo ignored his comment. Libra continued, "You must be very special to her all of a sudden."

Virgo clapped her hands. "Well Lancaster you're free now so go, run, get out of here and go find our Gems."

I raised my eyebrow. "Am I special to you?"

She raised her hand to slap me and I jumped back. She stomped her foot and pointed at a wall. "Get!"

"How can I leave by going through a wall?" I asked her.

She started pushing me toward the wall. I looked back and saw my dad with his eyes closed. He was fumbling his hands together. Cancer waved at me as I made it to the wall.

"Go through it." Virgo said.

"How?"

"Just walk through it." Virgo said slowly.

"But am I special to you?" I asked again.

"Get!" She pushed me through the wall.

As I was free falling in… let's just say deep space, I only saw darkness at first but then it was as if I was in a kaleidoscope. The colors blinded me so I kept my eyes closed. When I finally opened my eyes, I was surrounded by algebraic equations. Great… I was surrounded by my second worse fear (my first worse fear is… you know what, you don't need to know what it is). After passing the equations, I landed on a beach.

It wasn't like regular beaches with sand, an ocean, and beach volleyball. The sand was mud, the ocean was fire, and there was no beach volleyball. In fact, if I didn't see the Welcome to The Beach sign, I would not have known that it was a beach. I stood up but immediately fell back down. Now my entire backside was covered in mud. I stood up slower then looked around. The large consuming fire had the smell of heavy smoke in the air. I held my breath then walked along in the mud. I only fell five more times trying to walk in the mud. Each time I would slowly get back up then walk on. After what felt like hours, I made it to the end of the beach.

The smell of smoke changed into the smell of barbecue. Instead of seeing fire and mud, in the distance I saw a crystal blue ocean and pure white sand. The transition between the two beaches was amazing. I ran over to the actual beach slipping only twice. When I made it to the real beach, I saw two men. They each stood about twenty feet tall. One wore a blue tunic that was torched. The other wore a tunic made of fire. The man with the blue torched tunic had no mouth and the man with the fire tunic had no ears.

They each had a mark on their forehead. The one with no ears had a tattoo of a red snake on fire. The one with no mouth had a tattoo of a blue S surrounded by water. The earless man in the fire tunic laughed. His voice was deep and ominous. "Well, shall I strike first?" He said to the man with no mouth in the blue torched tunic.

The other man shrugged his shoulders.

The fire tunic man laughed again. "You fool." He said as he rushed the mouth less man.

The two men rushed towards each other and an explosion of fire and water erupted when they collided. The combination of the two elements caused an earthquake. I fell back into the sand as the ground rumbled. A giant sinkhole started to form on both sides. As I started to slip into the hole, I yelled for the two men to stop. The one with no mouth looked at me then ran over and picked me up in his hand just in time to save me.

He lifted up his hand to his eyes. I stood up and smiled. "Thank you, sir."

He nodded and looked over at the ocean. The other man ran to him and yelled in his ear, "Put that garbage down and fight me!" He pushed him to the ground. As his hand hit the sand, I was sent airborne straight to the fire ocean. Before I hit the fire, I saw a bright light. I closed my eyes, as the light got brighter.

When I opened my eyes, I was lying on a blanket on the ground. I sat up to see that I was in a library... a familiar looking library. It was Leo's library. I also saw a familiar looking girl. She was running her finger across the binding of each book on the bookshelves. She didn't see that I was awake so I cleared my throat.

Immediately her head turned and looked at me. She smiled and said. "Are you okay?"

I stood up. "Yeah, I'm okay. Where are the two fighting men from the beach and how did I get here?" She raised her eyebrow. "What two fighting men?"

I then realized that all of that was just a dream as I was falling in space. "Never mind, it was just a dream."

"Okay then." She walked over to me and put her hand on my shoulder. "Just for you to know, my dad doesn't like the fact that you're here so please try to ignore him."

I nodded. "Okay, no problem."

She bit her lip. "Ignore Calvin too."

"I thought he lived in a cave, does Calvin live here now."

"Not anymore." She sighed. "Wait here." She walked out the library.

I started looking around. I remembered the fireplace that Leo threw me into. I also remembered the book I saw, Dark Power: The Beast of Force. That one line I read rang in my ear, 'The Beast of Force still lives today and forever.' I browsed around to try to find the book. After searching for quite a bit I found it. I first looked around to make sure no one was in the room, and then I took the book. I picked up the blanket and rapped the book in it. Then I silently walked out the library with the book tucked under my arm.

My sneakers squeaked on the marble floor. I took them off to ensure that no one would hear me. Then I ran quickly and quietly trying to find the front door to leave. I was as quiet as a mouse as I search for the door. As I ran pass several paintings on the wall, I saw doors with the letter L in the center. The doors were made of cherry oak and smelled like oranges (not that I put my nose to each door and smelled them). As I ran the floors got more and more slippery as if they were just mopped. I ended up falling on the marble floors. I covered my mouth so no one could hear me yell. Then I stood up and brushed myself off.

"Who mops floors?" I asked myself. Then I heard Abigail's voice. There was someone else's voice too, a man's.

I opened the door that was beside me and ran in. I shut it quietly. The room had a huge indoor pool and a popcorn stand. It took everything in me to not eat the popcorn. I put my ear to the door to see if Abigail and the man were still there.

I heard Abigail laugh, saying. "He won't do us any harm."

"Yes, he will." The man said. "He has his father's Gem. Give him a tiny metal object and he can kill us all with a flex of his finger."

"He wouldn't do that. Look, just because you're mad doesn't mean that you can..."

"I'm not mad!" I heard a phone ringing. "Excuse me."

"Fine."

I waited five minutes then opened the door. I looked around and didn't see anyone for miles. So, I ran down the hallway to try to find the library again.

I finally got tired so I stopped running and sat down in front of a door that had a C instead of an L. I sighed and set my head against the door. I looked down at the book wrapped in the blanket. I removed the book from it and opened it. I sighed. This would be my second book I ever enjoyed to read (Zodiac Saga was the first book because I always believed in zodiac gods).

I was about to read the book, but then something or someone blocked my light. "Who are you?" I asked looking up.

The guy was in his early twenties. His blonde hair went to his slim shoulders. His eyes were the same color blue as his skinny jeans. His eyebrows were perfectly arched. His shirt was white like his teeth. "The question is, who are you?" He said extending his neck toward me. He spoke with a southern accent.

I stood up and covered the book with the blanket again tucking it under my arm. "I'm Lancaster."

He sighed in frustration. "Son of Aquarius?"

24

"Yeah."

He stomped his foot. "You're the one that invaded my home." He pushed me against the wall.

"Calvin, I didn't know I invaded your cave, I mean your home."

He rolled his eyes at me and started to yell. "Abigail! Abigail, come here!" He yelled. He tapped his foot impatiently. "I know you hear me! Come here!"

Abigail came running down the hallway and entered the room. "What?"

He pointed at me. "What is this and why is he here?"

She shook her head. "You mean who is this."

"Answer my question."

I raised my hand. "I told you I'm Lancaster... son of Aquarius."

He looked at me. "I wasn't talking to you." He looked back at Abigail. "Why is he here?"

She folded her arms. "Why don't you ask him all your questions?"

"Abigail, why is he here!"

"You don't have to yell. I'm right here and I can hear you."

He put his hand over his mouth. "I'm telling dad."

She laughed. "Wow. You're twenty-one years old and you're still tattling."

"Yes, that's right." Calvin said with a confident grin.

"Dad already knows he is here, so don't bother telling him."

"If dad already knows then why would you care if I tell him or not?"

She threw her hands up. "Fine, go tattle. When will you ever grow up, Calvin?"

"When I go bald and only then." He walked away whistling.

I looked at Abigail. "Hi."

She folded her arms. "I told you to stay in the library."

"I know but…"

She shook her head. "Find the door that has an A on it. The front door will be near there." She turned her back to me. "Oh, and by the way, you can keep the book and blanket." She said as she walked off.

I picked up my shoes and sighed. "This has been a very long day."

After searching and searching I found the front door. The doors were double doors and made of mahogany wood (I got an A in woodshop). Windows covered the top of the wooden doors. The handles were made of silver. I put my shoes back on my feet and opened the door. I walked out the house and shut the doors. I carefully walked down the white steps carefully. I touched the two stone lions that lied at the end of the white stairs. I walked along a circle driveway. Five cars scattered around the driveway. A black Mercedes Benz, a gray BMW, a pink Lamborghini, a red El Camino, and a white Dodge truck covered in mud. A fountain sat in the middle of the driveway. In the middle of the fountain was a sculpture of a lion standing up looking straight at me as water poured from its mouth. I turned around and saw that I wasn't just in a house… I was in a mansion. I was in a three-story mansion. On each of the front doors was the face of a lion roaring.

I laughed. "This is definitely Leo's house… mansion."

Then I heard a noise, the sound of a car cranking up and rock music playing. I turned and saw that someone was in the mud stained truck. The truck drove up beside me. The person put the window down which caused the rock music to blare louder. It was Calvin. He was wearing green sun glasses that had his name engraved on the sides.

He frowned and turned the music off. "Get in."

I backed up. "I'm not sure that's such a good idea."

"I have a legal driver's license. Get in the truck."

"Why would I get in?"

"You need a ride. Do you want to go to your friends or not?"

"Will you take me straight to them?" I asked.

"Son of Aquarius, get in the dang truck."

"Okay." I climbed in the truck and shut the door. I buckled my seatbelt and Calvin laughed.

"You use seatbelts?" He asked while laughing.

"Yes, I do wear seatbelts and you should buckle up too, now I mean it. I am a witness; it can protect you in a crash."

"Wow, okay, okay, whatever."

He pulled out of the driveway and a gate closed behind us. In less than thirty minutes the truck stopped. We arrived at a park and got into a parking spot to sit and look around. Calvin nodded his head and pointed forward. "There, your friends are over there somewhere."

"Right." I said. "So how do you know they're here?"

"The girl told me."

"What girl and did she send a silhouette?"

"I don't know and yeah it was a silhouette. Why?"

"No reason, I was Just wondering."

"Well good, now get out."

"Okay." I hopped out of the truck and shut the door. Immediately Calvin drove off.

"Thank you." I said as he continued driving off. I started walking forward and looked around. I saw moms sitting on benches watching their children play. I could smell barbeque in the distance and I could see the apples hanging high in the trees. I saw a little boy sitting on a branch in a tree. He was no more than seven years old. He had a bag beside him that he was filling with apples. He stopped when he saw me and smiled. I smiled back and he tossed me an apple. I caught it and smiled again then continued to walk forward. I only stopped walking when I heard a child scream. My head turned and I saw Judas holding a little boy by the arm. The boy was screaming to the top of his lungs and yet Judas didn't let go.

I ran as fast as I could over to Judas. I was only about ten feet away from him when someone tackled me from the side. I hit the ground headfirst. The apple flew out of my hand I lay down on the ground for about ten seconds. I opened my eyes and looked up. The little boy that was being held by Judas was no longer crying. I stood up and held my head as I limped over to Judas. When I got closer, I saw that the boy wasn't crying anymore because he was dead.

"Judas, what have you done!" I yelled.

He turned to me and dropped the little boy to the ground. Judas shook his head and his eyes started to glow. He pointed at me and once again I was tackled to the ground. I hit the ground headfirst again. This time before the person left, I grabbed their throat. The person punched my nose and I got a massive nosebleed. The person stood and held their hand out as if they wanted to help me up. I tilted my head down and put my hand under my nose. I accepted the stranger's help. Now that I was standing, I could see who it was. It was Sofia.

I sighed. "You broke my nose, why did you do that?!"

Sofia laughed. "You grabbed my neck so I broke your nose!"

"You tackled me thrice so I grabbed your neck! Just stop tackling me" I yelled at her.

She stood up. "Where's the apple you had?"

"Why were you tackling me?!" I yelled back loudly.

She pointed for me to look at Judas. "The apples on these trees were created by Gemini. When you eat one or hold one a silhouette will possess you. I kept tackling you because someone was throwing the apples and the silhouettes were escaping from the apples."

"Wait, the apples can possess people?" I asked as I was wiping my blood from my nose on my pants.

"Yes. But these silhouettes can only be out of the apples for ten seconds every ten thousand years, unless they are inside of a body. So, they possess bodies."

"So, when silhouettes come close to a human, they leave the apples and control them so they can be free." I said trying to understand and catching on.

She nodded. "Now one of them is possessing Judas, see."

"Okay, okay I see him and I understand now. We need help, where's Peter?"

"Helping the people."

"Wait a minute. Did a little boy in a tree give Judas that apple, he gave me my apple also?"

Her eyes widened. "Yes, now stay here." She ran off.

"Wait! Bring me back a bandage!" I yelled to her. I turned over to where Judas was. He was gone and I sighed. I looked to my left and saw an army of people walking in a straight line.

As I looked at them, I was afraid. About twenty apples flew toward me. I started to run. I turned around and saw the silhouettes leaving the apples and flying toward me. I counted down: ten, nine, eight, seven, six, five, four, three, two… on two they all sped up. I jumped down on the ground and they all disappeared above my head. I looked up and saw that the straight line of people stopped and ran toward me.

I got up and looked around. Then I saw monkey bars. Perfect. I held out my hand and rapped the monkey bars around the people using my dad's gem to control metal. I missed some of the people so they ran after me. I ran away from them. I ran and hid behind a tree... full of apples. That wasn't a genius move. At least fifty silhouettes flew toward me. I ran as fast as my sore legs could go.

I was almost safe until something cliché happened. I tripped on an apple and fell flat on my face. I turned on my back and saw a silhouette hovering over me. Then... everything went black. My eyes opened and I saw nothing but darkness. I yelled and heard nothing but a faint echo of my voice. I saw a glow of purple and I ran toward it. I stopped when I saw that it was a silhouette. It stared at me motionless.

I felt my nose and saw that it was no longer bleeding. "Stop controlling my body." I yelled at the silhouette. Its purple figure still didn't move. I ran toward It and threw punches at It, but my fist went through It. I tried to grab at It, but It was like a ghost. I tried punching it again and then realized something. The Aquarius gem was gone. The Gem was no longer on my wrist. There was nothing there but a scar.

"What did you do with my Aquarius gem?!" I yelled at the silhouette.

It still didn't move.

I sat down in front of It and sighed. I closed my eyes. "Dad, if you can hear me, I need your help. Please, help me." I opened my eyes and saw that It had Its head cocked to the side. "What?" I asked It.

It straightened Its head and flung back into the darkness. I stood up and walked in Its path towards it. As I walked on mist covered the ground. The mist soon turned into thick marshy water. I stopped and sighed. "Dad! Gemini! Sofia! Someone help me!" I rolled up my pants legs and kept walking through the water.

I finally stopped walking when I heard a noise. Someone or something was singing. It sounded soft and beautiful. It put me in a trance. I couldn't control myself. I smiled and ran toward the singing. I saw that the singing was coming from the silhouette.

It was floating just above the water. As It sang Its purple eyes glowed. I smiled bigger and walked to It. It reached It's hand out to me. I was about to put my hand in It's, but I heard something else.

I heard a voice in my head say, "Don't do that. If you do then you and the silhouette will forever be one. Wet the silhouette using the water, then grab It and don't let go no matter what." The voice said. Then the voice went away.

It sang louder and extended Its hand more to me. I smiled at It. Then in a flash I laid my hand in the water and threw water up to wet it. It did an ear-piercing scream and I yelled in pain. Then I remembered what the voice said. I grabbed it and didn't let go (I followed what the voice said because I knew better then to not listen to random things like that). It kicked and screamed louder but I didn't let go.

It flew high above the water but I still didn't let go. I rapped my entire body around It and we started to fall. We landed in the water and the screaming stopped. I looked and saw that It was gone. I stood up soaked in water. I shook my wet hair.

Then an object with a silver light appeared in the water. I grabbed the object in the water and the darkness started to disappear. I saw orange and realized that the sun was setting. I also realized that I was still in the park and people were still possessed. The Aquarius Gem was back on my wrist and a purple silhouette was lying beside me as if It was unconscious. I put my hand on It and Its body twitched. I stood up and scooped the silhouette up in my arms.

I saw another army of people walking in a straight line. I started walking toward the parking lot. All of the cars were half destroyed. I heard footsteps behind me and saw that it was the little boy that was in the tree. He shook his head. "I don't understand. When I gave you the apple the silhouette should've inhabited you, but it didn't. It doesn't make sense. Unless the silhouette that was in that apple was already gone."

I set the silhouette down and looked at the cars around me. "Who are you?" I asked the boy.

"Someone who is following orders."

"Orders from who?"

He pulled an apple from his bag. "You hungry?"

"Answer me!" I said very loudly.

"Really, take this apple. It's quite delicious."

I held my hand out and used the Aquarius gem to ram the little boy with the cars from the parking lot. I watched as his blood went everywhere. Then I smiled when I saw that he was dead. I picked the silhouette up again and started to walk. I walked until it was night. I was out of the park and sitting at a bus stop. I sat on the bench and laid the silhouette beside me. I folded my hands together and sighed.

Why didn't the silhouette leave the apple when I held it? Was it because there wasn't one in it or because it just didn't want to mess with me? I looked down at the silhouette and Its body twitched again. I twiddled my thumbs for a while then stood. I picked It up and It flew out of my arms. Its eyes started glowing again. I backed up and It held It's hand out to me. The voice came in my head again saying. "Go ahead. It can't possess you now." Then the voice in my head went away.

I put my hand in Its hand and I got a rush of adrenaline. I saw nothing but blue and green lights rushing in front of me. Then I saw my dad, Aquarius. I was standing in the middle of the throne room in the Temple of Zodia. I then saw the rest of the Elders. None of them were smiling… except for Cancer, as always. He was eating a burrito and drinking an extra-large drink.

He took a bite of his burrito and smiled at me again saying. "Hi Lancaster!"

Gemini slapped him in the back of the head. "Shut up Cancer!"

Aquarius shook his head. "Lancaster, this is the second time today you have come here."

"We should've killed him." Taurus said.

Libra looked at Gemini. "I curse the day you invented those apples. By tomorrow the city of Seattle will be controlled by those things."

Gemini shrugged her shoulders. "Let's let our little adventurers stop them." She said pointing at me.

I raised my hand. "Why did you create those apples anyway?"

She sighed. "When my idiot brother lost our Gems, I created those apples so that my silhouettes could inhabit them. When they would inhabit them, I would place them on a tree and have them look to see if my Gem was anywhere near their location. After thousands of years of not being around me, the silhouettes grew independent. So now they have their own free will."

I scratched my head. "So, you created millions of apples for your silhouettes to live in. Then you put them in trees in various locations in hopes of finding your Gem."

"Right, she said."

With puzzling thoughts, I said "Why don't you get them back?!"

She rolled her eyes. "Because they're independent now."

"How can you not control what you created?" I said as I scratch my head really trying to understand.

"Stop." Virgo interrupted. She looked over at Aquarius. "Your son is just like you."

"I know." Aquarius folded his arms proudly.

"Gemini, can't you at least try to stop your silhouettes?" I asked.

"Stop." Virgo said with more force before Gemini could reply.

"Okay." I responded. "Can you guys send me back now?" They didn't respond to me because their attention was focused and looking behind me.

"Now what?" I turned and saw the silhouette floating behind me.

Gemini stood up from her throne in shock. She tried to bring the silhouette to her. "It won't come to me. Lancaster, what did you do to it?"

"Well, it's a long story but here is the short of it." So, I told them all about me going to the park (though I didn't tell them that Calvin drove me there) and all about the boy in the tree, Judas, me in the dark place, me killing the boy, the water, and the silhouette teleporting me there.

Gemini shook her head and leaned forward. She looked at Pisces. "Why the water?"

Pisces folded his arms. "It wasn't regular water. It had all kinds of spells and potions in it. Someone somewhere is finding our weaknesses and using them against us. That can be dangerous for the entire universe."

"How did you know that the water had potions and spells?" Virgo asked him.

"Because of what Lancaster said. Gemini's silhouettes have been in water before without any affects. They are accustomed to outside elements. Plus, that girl with her Gem has probably had her silhouettes in the rain and she hasn't told us that yet."

Virgo nodded. "So, someone is finding our weaknesses… great."

Cancer smiled. "What's your weakness Virgo?"

"Gemini, what do we do about that silhouette." Virgo said pointing at the one behind me.

"It's contaminated so I don't know." Gemini responded.

I smiled. "Can I keep It with me?"

Aquarius laughed and shook his head. "Well Gemini, can he keep It?"

Taurus stood. "Why would you want to keep that thing?"

"Taurus, sit down." Gemini commanded. Taurus did as she said. Gemini looked at me. "He can keep my silhouette if It allows him to." She said slowly.

I turned to It and held out my hand. "You want to stay with me?"

It looked at my hand for a few seconds. Then It responded how I wanted it to. It put it hand in mine and again I saw blue and green colors rushing pass me as I fall asleep.

A Return in Time

I opened my eyes and saw Sofia standing over me. She sighed. "You're so stupid." She helped me up. "Did you really think that silhouette would stay with you?"

We were standing in the middle of a vacant parking garage. Graffiti covered all of the walls and trash covered the ground.

I shrugged my shoulders. "Yeah I guess."

She rolled her eyes. "You really are stupid, and you're lucky I like you."

"You already said that I am stupid, wait, you like me."

"Just shut up, I said no such thing." She said with a shy smile.

Okay, whatever. So, where's Peter and… Judas?" I asked.

"About ten minutes ago Peter went to find you." She shook her head. "Judas is still being controlled by the silhouettes."

"Well, whenever the silhouette controlled me, it sang some type of song. Then a voice came in my head and told me to put some type of special water on It. That's how I got free from it."

Her eyes widened. "Did you recognize the voice?"

"No, I did not, but I think it may have sounded familiar but am not sure."

"Was it a male or female voice?"

"Definitely a male voice."

"And you did as the voice said even though you didn't know who it was?" Sofia sarcastically said to me.

"Yeah and I wasn't under the silhouette control after I did as the voice said."

"Come on, let's go find Peter." Sofia said.

"Okay." I said eyeing an old rusty metal bottle cap. I picked it up and put it in my pocket.

When we found Peter ten guys had him surrounded. They all looked to be around his age and wore orange prison uniforms covered by denim jackets. They each had their own weapon. Three of the men had baseball bats, four had knives, two had crowbars, and one had a revolver pistol.

"Stay down, stay quiet and follow me." Sofia whispered to me. She ran behind the closest building to the men and crouched down.

I ran up behind her and crouched down too. I carefully listened to what was happening. "Shouldn't we help?"

"Shut up." Sofia warned.

"Give us your money!" The man with the revolver said. He had the name Luther tattooed on his arm. "Give me the cash now!"

Peter sighed. "I don't have any money."

"Stop lying'!" One of the baseball bat holders yelled. "Everyone carries money, so give it up now!"

"Not me." Peter said smiling.

The gun holder put the gun to Peter's head. "You got five seconds."

Peter shrugged. "I can't count." The man started to count down slowly.

I nudged Sofia. "Let me do something!" I yelled. I immediately covered my mouth. I said that louder than I wanted to.

Sofia punched my stomach. "When will you listen?!" She turned and saw that the men were looking down at us. She rolled her eyes. "Great." Then suddenly, ten silhouettes fell from the sky, grabbed the men, and dragged them down into the ground.

"Where did the silhouettes take them?" I asked clutching my stomach.

She punched my throat and rolled her eyes. "Shut up!" She left my line of sight and walked off.

I grabbed my throat and coughed. I walked in Sofia's direction to find that her and Peter were gone. I looked and searched around but they were gone. So, I was left alone in a place that I had no idea about how to get out of. I took the metal bottle cap out of my pocket and set it on the ground. "Focus," I told myself as I gazed at the bottle cap intensely.

I closed my eyes and took a deep breath. I kept focusing for several more seconds. When I opened my eyes, what happened was what I wanted to happen. The metal bottle cap expanded enough for me to stand on it. I stood on the expanded metal and it started to float then fly through the air. I rubbed my sore throat as I flew over rooftops.

I kept flying until my battle against fatigue ended. Fatigue won. My eyes closed ever so slowly. I then felt wind rush pass my ears. A ringing sound in my ear as I opened my eyes. I was free falling in the air. I bit my tongue so I wouldn't yell.

I was about three feet from the ground when all of a sudden, I stopped falling. I heard a girl giggling behind me. I imagined it was Sofia but I knew better than to believe that Sofia would ever laugh like that. I fell down but not hard to the ground. I stood up and brushed myself off. It was Mercy.

"Mercy, what are you doing here?" I said trying not to reveal the anger in my voice. After all, she was the one that almost got Taurus to kill me.

She hugged me. "I know you're really upset with me…"

"Enraged is more like it." I said pushing her away.

"I know." She said looking down. "But I want to repay you."

"If you really want to repay me, you'll leave me alone." I insisted.

She shook her head and grinned. "Will you come with me?" She asked sincerely.

I thought about it for a few seconds. "Why should I go anywhere with you?"

She folded her arms. "Because, I can either take you to your friends or to your father."

"My father? Why would you take me to him?"

She looked down again. "Because... he's in... danger."

"What?" I said surprisingly. "What's going on?"

"Taurus." She said slowly and silently.

"Take me to my father." I said without asking anymore questions.

"Your friend Judas is causing trouble on the other side of town. That's why Peter and Sofia left you."

I sat on the ground. "So, I can either save my dad or save my friends?"

She nodded yes slowly.

I scratched my head vigorously and grunted. "Sofia and Peter can handle Judas. Take me to my father."

Mercy teleported me back to the Temple of Zodia. We were at the entrance of the garden. The aroma of plants and flowers filled the air as we walked through. Virgo was conjuring up little water pots.

She glanced at us. "They're over there." She said pointing ahead.

"What happened?" I asked Virgo while accidentally stepping in a puddle of water.

Vines crawled up behind her and formed a chair. She sat down still allowing the plants and flowers to be watered. "Taurus was in the throne room still upset about you nearly killing his daughter."

"It wasn't me trying to kill Mercy, it was…"

Virgo held up her hand for me to stop talking. She started to speak saying "Aquarius went into the throne room to talk to Taurus about you and Mercy. When he tried to tell Taurus, you did not try to kill Mercy, Taurus got more enraged and now they're fighting again."

I turned to Mercy. "Thanks a lot, Mercy. You can straighten this whole thing out by telling your father the truth. Just tell him you were trying to kill Sofia and I just stopped you."

She shrugged her shoulders and said nothing back to me. "Why would they fight here?" She asked Virgo, still totally ignoring my plea for her to tell the truth.

Virgo rolled her eyes. "Because, Libra told them that if they want to fight, they have to fight here. So here it is."

"Why here?" I asked, now forgetting about pleading to Mercy for her to be honest with Taurus.

"You will need to ask Libra why fight here." Virgo stood. "Go stop them. They are ruining the mood for me."

"Who go stop them? "

"Because you two caused this whole misunderstanding, you two are going."

"No, we didn't." I said. "Only Mercy lied and caused this misunderstanding. And I know it was on purpose!

Mercy sighed. "My father isn't the one who wanted to fight."

"Really, well if you don't stop them from fighting, I will fight you, how about that!" I warned.

"Stop, quiet." Virgo said in annoyance.

"Why don't you stop them… mother." Mercy asked smiling.

"Because I didn't cause this."

"But you helped stop them from arguing before." I reminded her.

"That doesn't mean I'll help now." Virgo said gently.

"Well you should." I said in an unrest tone.

"I should… but I won't."

Virgo waved her hands and vines started to crawl over next to me. They formed a sword. "Pick it up." Virgo said.

I picked it up and grunted as it stuck into my right hand. My hand started bleeding and it hurt. "That sword purposefully cut me and it hurts!?"I yelled out at Virgo.

Virgo took one of the water pots and put it under my hand. It caught my blood and the pot turned from green to red. She moved the pot and my hand stopped bleeding. The pain went away also.

Virgo smiled to herself, as if I wasn't looking. "Go fight Taurus." She commanded me. She turned to Mercy. "You just stay here. Apparently, we have a lot to talk about concerning your little story about what happened at the hospital."

Mercy nodded okay. "Sure, I understand."

Virgo pushed me. "Now go, stop the fight."

I didn't stay and argue with them. I walked in the direction Virgo pointed me to go. The cut from the sword was causing my hand to itch. It felt like an allergic reaction with a rash. It was impossible to scratch the area and get relief so I had to try to take my mind off of it.

As I kept walking, I tried thinking about Peter and Sofia trying to save Judas. No doubt other people who were under the silhouettes control will be with Judas also. I started thinking that maybe I should've stayed and help save my friends instead. I stopped thinking when I saw a figure coming towards me and fell down in front of me. It was my father, Aquarius. I screamed in surprise and looked down at him. His red tunic was damp with water and his skin oozing a black substance.

I knelt down in front of him. "Dad?"

His eyes opened slowly moving up and down. He struggled and sat up and put his head in his hands. He looked at me and said one word, "Run!"

I then saw Taurus running toward us like a battering ram. I stood up and jumped in front of my dad. I did not run. I sighed and closed my eyes. When my eyes were closed, I saw blue mist and the water pot Virgo used to catch my blood when the sword cut my hand.

The silhouette that tried to control me was holding the water pot as if its life depended on it. Virgo stood behind It and whispered something but I could not hear her. A green light appeared in front of them. The two got on their knees and put their faces to the ground. The silhouette pushed the watering pot to the light. The light expanded and my eyes opened.

I saw my dad sitting in a chair beside a bed I was in. He was no longer oozing whatever he was oozing. His tunic was now orange. He ran his hand through his dark brown hair. His eyes closed and he sighed. I scratched my head and observed my surroundings. I was in a small room with yellow walls and it smelled like bubble gum. The bed sheets were covered in what appeared to be grass stains.

"What happened?" I asked my dad, Aquarius. He didn't respond or move.

"Dad?" I shook his shoulder. "Are you okay? What happened?"

He sat back in the chair. He set his elbow on the arm of the chair and rested his head on his fist.

"Say something to me!" I finally said.

He opened his eyes and sat forward. "What do you want me to say to you?!" He said in a tone I never heard him use before.

"Ask me if I'm okay, just say something to me!" I said in the same tone.

He shook his head. "Mercy nearly got you killed and yet you decided to trust her!"

"I trusted her because I wanted to save you! I needed her to bring me here to save you."

"Well you didn't!" He stood up. "I told you to run but you didn't!"

I got out of the bed. "I didn't listen and run because Taurus was trying to kill you!"

He stomped his foot. "That was the point!" He closed his eyes and exhaled softy. "I was the distraction. While I was distracting Taurus, Sagittarius would come and shoot him with a sleeping arrow." He opened his eyes. "Then we would cast him out of the temple like we did Cancer." My head dropped in sadness.

"And now I have ruined the plan because I didn't listen when you said run?"

"Yes."

"The last thing I remember is Taurus charging at you and I closed my eyes. What happened after that?" I asked again in a quiet tone.

"When you closed your eyes, your sword flew out of your hand and went toward Sagittarius not Taurus. Sagittarius dodged the sword and his sleeping arrow hit you. That's why you were here in bed asleep. That gave Taurus the opportunity to escape us."

My eyes widened. "Oh. Well the plan still worked; Taurus is gone."

"Yes, but he is gone out into the world. And we wouldn't have cast him out into the world like we did Cancer. The plan was to put him in isolation and not out into the world." He shook his head in disappointment. "And why would your sword attack Sagittarius and not Taurus?"

"I don't know but Virgo made me that sword. She probably used magic or…"

"I've heard enough, take a look at your right hand."

I did as he said and looked at my right hand. My hand had little dots on it where the sword had cut me. The dots formed a V. "V for Virgo." I said under my breath.

"Now look at your wrist, what's missing."

I looked at my left wrist. "Oh no, where's the Aquarius Gem?"

He held out his hand and the Gem appeared. "You'll get this back when you learn how to listen."

"But it's mine…"

"No, there are no buts about it and it's not yours. Because of you a Zodian with incredible strength is on the loose in the world. Now we have to find him and put him away."

"Sofia will not like it when she finds out about this. She will not understand why her father is being hunted" I said in a quiet concerning voice. I was also thinking about how her and Peter are doing with Judas.

"The Elders and I can defend against Sofia even though she has a Gem." Then the Gem in Aquarius's hand disappeared. "Now son, even though I took the Gem away from you that doesn't mean you can stop searching for the other gems. So, get back to searching for the gems. I will take you back to your friends in the Zodian helicopter."

"Okay, but I promise to listen, so will you please give me back the gem. Come on give it back. I'll learn to listen."

"Yes, you will learn to listen and no I will not give it back now."

"Give me the Gem!" I yelled without thinking.

"Do not command me!" Aquarius walked to the door. "I am your father and you are my son. You will treat me with respect!"

"And if I don't?"

He turned to me and sighed. "Then may the son of Scorpio take your soul. Now let's go, now." He said in such a voice that I started to shake as we boarded the helicopter.

There were twelve throne seats to choose from. I sat behind my father as he piloted the jet-black machine that glided along the sky. My headset weighed heavily on the top of my head. I was surrounded by luxury and felt like we were standing still and not moving. My dad was quiet but I knew I needed to say something. I didn't want my last words to him to be 'and if I don't'.

"Hey… dad…" I said in an apologetic tone hoping to break the ice with him.

He was quiet and sat comfortably still as he flew the Zodian helicopter. The smooth ride was rhythmic and relaxing. I tapped my feet and twisted my lips. What do I say to him to start a conversation? Ask him what it's like to be a god? Ask him how things were before mortals came? Does he like sports? Would he take me to a game one day? Peter taught me how to throw a football and baseball, but I was never cut-out for a team. Maybe Aquarius made himself a sports player and became a big star?

"Hey, dad? I said again in a sincere voice. What was it like coming to earth for the first time?"

"Disappointing." He said shortly and almost too quickly, as if to send a silent message for me to stay quiet.

"Like me?"

He was quiet and said nothing else in response.

I was quiet and said nothing else on the ride.

We finally landed back in Seattle. When he landed the helicopter, I stepped out and walked off without looking back and he didn't say a word. The helicopter flew off and I sighed as I looked up at it flying away. I begin to search around and immediately noticed I got back too late. Everyone in the city seemed to be under the silhouettes control.

Finally, as I kept searching, I found Sofia and Peter but they were engaged in a battle, with each other. Sofia caught sight of me and ran in my direction with Peter chasing after her. Thankfully she was not under the control of the silhouettes because she had a gem. Peter was a different story; he was possessed by the silhouette.

When Sofia reached me, she grabbed onto my shirt and said "run "dragging me with her. I remembered the last person who told me to 'run' I didn't listen. It was my dad. I stumbled as she was dragging and pulling me backwards. When I saw Peter closing in and picking up speed, I turned around and ran faster.

"What happened to you?" Sofia asked me out of breath as we run.

"I'll sum it up for you quickly. Mercy took me to my dad. By not listening I ruined a plan he and Sagittarius had to capture Taurus, your dad. As punishment to me, he took away the Aquarius gem and brought me back here." I told her in quick short breaths.

"What? What plan between him and Sagittarius and why capture my dad?"

Now that there was some distance between Peter and us, I slowed my running down to slow my speech down. "There was a plan to take Taurus to an isolated secret place where he wouldn't be able to hurt anybody."

She suddenly stopped running completely and looked confused. "Wait, they wanted to put my daddy, Taurus, in isolation? Why?" Her eyes widened.

I put my hand on her shoulder. "I messed up so they didn't capture him. He is still free."

Sofia reached up to move my hand from her shoulder and noticed a mark on my hand. She looked intensely at my hand. "What is that, is that a V?"

"V for Virgo." Sofia had a look of disbelief and disgust on her face.

She threw my hand down and turned to walk off. "Duck."

"No, you got it right the first time; it is a V for Virgo not Duck?" I said back to her.

"Duck!" She tackled me to the ground just as Peter flew over our heads.

He landed on his feet and ran after us again. His eye sockets were empty and deep. A bow and arrow appeared in his hands. He fired an arrow toward us and a silhouette blocked it.

Sofia started running again. "Come on, run, he is possessed!" She yelled back at me.

I took off running and caught up to her. "Why are we running? Just use your Gem silhouette to fight him."

"It won't work. Those silhouettes are stronger than the silhouette from my Gem." She said tiredly and out of breath.

In a quick hush of a moment, as we kept running, she looked over at me as if she was looking right through me and sighed with relief. Then she said to me "If I tell you something will you keep it a secret?"

I gulped. I honestly didn't know whether or not to say yes. I imagined it wasn't a secret that other girls her age would have. "Sure. Yeah, I will keep a secret for you."

"I know where my daddy is hiding." She said in a happy whisper voice.

"How do you know where he is hiding? Did he tell you?"

"No. I just know somehow." We slowly stopped running. "Look!" She said pointing ahead.

There were several more people under the silhouettes' control and they were running toward us. Peter was still shooting arrows at us. Soon the crowd of possessed people had us surrounded.

I closed my eyes and wanted to pray; I knew we needed help. "We need help and we need it now?" I said in a very nervous voice as I looked around at the crowd.

Sofia sighed and without an eye roll she yelled. "Daddy, daddy!" She said yelling to the top of her lungs. Nothing happened. She took a deep breath and yelled again to the top of her lungs. "Daddy, daddy!" She yelled again and again each time louder.

Then I saw a roll of dust as the ground rumble beneath us. In the distance I heard a familiar battle cry sound getting closer and closer. With the force of an earthquake Taurus landed in front of us. The impact of the landing made the crowd and I fall to the ground, but not Sofia. I imagined she didn't fall because she was used to him doing that.

At once the possessed crowd started to flee from us. Taurus picked up one of the possessed people. He swung them above his head using them as a weapon to wipe out what was left of the crowd. As for Peter, he ran off with the other possessed.

When Taurus was done clearing the possessed crowd, he turned to Sofia. "Samantha." "Are you alright?" He picked her up with a big bear hug then set her down.

"I'm fine daddy." She said glancing back at me. "I don't want them to take you away." She told him.

With a look of shame Taurus turned looking away from her. He then finally caught sight of me. "It's you, Lancaster!" He picked me up until I was eye level with him. His denim eyes widened. "You saved me from being captured."

"About that..." I started. "I accidently saved you from capture. I didn't know they were trying to capture you." After I said that I realized that I should've just kept my mouth shut.

He dropped me to the ground. "What do you mean, you accidently saved me?"

I stood up and rubbed my backside. "I mean just that, I wasn't trying to save you, I was trying to save my father from you. But the sword that Virgo gave me attacked Sagittarius instead of you." I didn't tell him about what I saw when I closed my eyes because... well... he's Taurus.

Taurus shook his head and turned to Sofia. "First, he tries to kill you, and then he helps me escape and says it was an accident to help me. Why do you still stay around him?"

She sighed. "This was all Mercy's doing, daddy. Lancaster did not try and kill me, it was Mercy. He tried to get Mercy to save me after she cut my throat."

He scratched his light brown goatee. "If this is true then why haven't you told Virgo the truth? Why haven't you told me and the others?"

"Because, Virgo and Mercy are probably in on it together. Remember what Pisces said, someone is trying to find the Elder's weaknesses." I said.

He smiled and then laughed. "And you think that Virgo would turn against us? If anyone would turn against us it would be Scorpio." He joked.

Sofia grabbed her father's arm. "Mercy would certainly do it." She said softly.

He picked up his daughter and held her as if she was six years old. "Come on Samantha, we have things to take care of."

Her mouth hung open then closed as if she knew what he meant. She nodded and looked at me. "Stay safe, I have to go."

Taurus sighed and jumped into the air with Sofia in his arms. They were gone. I looked around at the fallen people. They started to rise to their feet. Some had no eyeballs some did. The ones that did were free. The ones that were free ran off and I did the same.

I ran as fast as I could. "Think Lancaster. Think. You need to find a place to hide." I looked around but saw nowhere safe to hide. All of the buildings were locked and the alleys were not safe.

I picked up speed running until I saw a familiar white truck coming toward me. It looked like Calvin's truck. I slowed down and stepped off to the side to wait for the truck to get closer. The truck slowed down and the door opened. Without thinking, I jumped in the truck without feeling fear.

I closed the door, rolled up the window, and put on my seatbelt. I sighed in relief. Without looking at the driver I said "Thanks Calvin, you are a life saver."

"I'm not Calvin." The driver said angrily. "And if anyone else would have called me Calvin I would have killed them."

Looking over at the driver I said "Oh… sorry… thanks Abigail. I just assumed… wait where's Calvin?"

She tapped the steering wheel. "He's somewhere, I guess."

"Obviously he is somewhere." I smiled "Anyway, what are you doing here, oh and thank you?"

"Shoot!" She swerved passed some people. They started running after the truck. Abigail looked in the rearview mirror. "Use that Gem of yours to levitate the truck." She said in a hasty voice.

"One: my dad took away the Gem. Two: even if I had the Gem the truck would be too hard for me." I told her.

"Your dad took his Gem from you?!" She swerved passed more people.

"Yeah, he took it from me. I don't want to talk about it." I looked through the side mirror. "Don't you have your father's Gem?"

"No. Calvin had it but lost it in a game of poker."

I smirked. "He lost Leo's Gem in a game of poker?"

"Yeah, can you believe it. He's grounded for a while."

"Where are you taking me?" I asked. She tapped the steering wheel again. "Out of Seattle for sure. Everyone in the entire city is under the silhouettes control."

"Wait, didn't Gemini put the apples in other locations?"

She swerved. "Yeah, but maybe those locations haven't gone rogue yet like Seattle. At least I hope not."

She looked at me. "What are we supposed to do about them, Lancaster? How can we get rid of them?" All of a sudden, we heard a loud boom and the entire truck shook. Abigail screamed and the air bags deployed. The air bag hit my face and suffocated me. I lost the ability to move. I could only scream, but my scream was muffled. I closed my eyes and saw someone.

I saw a person wearing a red hooded robe. They held a scythe in their right hand and a book in their left. They were surrounded by chaos and they were laughing.

The voice was gentle but their appearance, was anything but gentle. "It's not your time… at least not yet." The book opened and a green glow came into view. The water pot Virgo put my blood in floated next to the book.

The person sighed. The robe changed to black and their voice changed from gentle to a more ominous tone. Each word they spoke produced thunder. "For the sake of this world, may the end of days cease until our subjugator is revealed."

Lightning flashed and I was lying in the truck. I rubbed my eyes and looked at my hands. I realized that my face was covered in blood. Abigail lay unconscious in the driver's seat. She too was covered in blood only she wasn't moving. The possessed people had caught up to the truck. The people banged on the truck much like a criminal would bang on a jail cell wall. I saw a little boy standing on the hood of the truck. He was the same boy in the tree from the park. He kicked the already broken windshield until it was completely shattered. He looked at me and shook his head. "You should've stayed under the silhouette control."

"And you should've stayed dead." I fired back saying to the boy. "Just leave us alone."

"Us?" He asked.

I pointed at Abigail who still hadn't moved. I sighed. "Help us, you are not possessed, you are still human so help us."

He motioned the possessed people to stop banging on the truck and move back. I scratched my wrist and then behind my ear.

"Like I told you before, I'm just following orders." The boy said cold heartedly.

"From who? Gemini? Taurus? Virgo? Who?" I knew that Zodians used people to do evil works but a child? "It is just not right; you are a child and you are still human. You should not be used to do evil like this. Tell me who you are taking orders from, please."

Hearing those words caused the look on the boy's face to change. He licked his lips in thought. "I'm taking orders from… AH!" Before he could finish, he had an arrow in his heart. He fell back off the truck windshield and the possessed people looked down at him in shock.

Someone jumped on the roof of the truck. I thought it was Peter so I closed my eyes and hoped for the best.

"Open your eyes!" A roaring voice said.

I jumped and opened my eyes. I saw something in front of me with the head of a lion and the body of a bear. My eyes widened. "Leo?"

He reached in through the windshield and picked up his daughter Abigail's lifeless body and roared at the possessed people around us. They all ran off in terror. He roared at me as he looked over. "We should've killed you." He stepped down off the truck with Abigail in his arms.

"No, no, wait!" I climbed through the windshield behind them. "You are not leaving me! I'm sick of everyone leaving me at the worse times!"

He changed his body into a cheetah and Abigail sat loosely on his back. "Your friend is about to shoot an arrow at you." Leo said as he ran off with Abigail.

I didn't bother to turn around, I knew it was Peter. I just quickly ducked down and an arrow flew over my head. Then I turned around and looked at Peter. "Okay, you're making me do this." I ran at him with my head level with his stomach. My head hit his stomach and we both fell to the ground. I punched his face repeatedly over and over again. The bow and arrow flew out of Peter's hand and vanished. He grunted and pushed me off of him. His face was covered in bruises. The silhouette flew out of him and hit the ground. The silhouette slowly disappeared and went away in a series of screams. Peter rose to his knees and clenched his stomach.

He looked up at me. "What happened?"

"Long story short, you got controlled by a silhouette that went rogue."

"What happened to your face?"

I wiped some of the blood off my face. "Car accident."

"But you are okay, right?" He asked rising to his feet.

"Yeah, I'm fine." I patted his shoulder. I was glad someone cared about me.

He grabbed my wrist looking curiously. "Where's the Aquarius Gem?"

"Let's just say the gem owner took it back."

"Why did your dad take it?"

"I don't want to talk about it." I rubbed my carved hand looking at the V. "Everyone in the city is under control of the silhouettes."

"The rogue ones, yeah I remember now. We have to go."

"Where and how? We have no transportation… and we're out of time." I said pointing behind Peter. More people were coming.

Peter held out his hands and his bow emerged accompanied with a quiver full of arrows. "Need to time this just right." He aimed his bow then closed his eyes and released an arrow. The impact resembled a nuclear bomb. His eyes opened. "Let's go." We ran away quickly.

I ran behind him not knowing or worrying about where we were going. I was sick of running and tired of these silhouettes. I was also sick of everyone leaving me. I was sick of everything. I planned on trying to convince Gemini into at least trying to stop her silhouettes. If she didn't listen then... then I would keep worrying, I guess.

According to Abigail the other silhouettes didn't go insane. It is the ones in the poison apples. Maybe soon they will too. I was also sick of that little boy. I killed him, then he came back, then he was killed again. Will he come back again? Before he told me who he was working for Peter shot him with an arrow. Will I ever find out?

Peter stopped running when we turned a corner and saw a familiar face lying on the ground. "Judas!"

His red shirt was torn in various places. His black pants were covered in blood like his arms. His red high tops were chained together. He moaned and slowly placed his hands on his forehead.

His crimson eyes opened. "I feel... terrible."

Peter laughed. "Glad you're still here." He helped Judas up from the ground.

Judas looked down. "Why are my feet chained together?"

"We Don't know." I said now coming into his view.

"Lancaster! Dude I thought the Zodians killed you. What happened to your face?"

"Car accident, what happened to you?"

"Oh yeah, what did happen to me?"

"Gemini's poison apples happened to you." Peter said.

Judas nodded. "Oh. I see." He sighed. "So, can you two help me get this chain off my feet?"

It was dawn by the time the three of us exited the city. Peter and Judas were tired but I surprisingly still had energy. Judas finally stopped walking and collapsed on the ground.

He stretched out his body and yawned. "Let's take a break." His eyes closed immediately.

"I agree." Peter said lying down. "You should sleep to Lancaster." His eyes closed also.

"Okay, maybe I will." I sat down and sighed.

In one day, an entire city was under the control of rogue silhouettes. The maker of the silhouettes won't try to help the city. Soon other cities will be the same way. I scratched my wrist and observed my hand. The V looked darker and deeper. Feeling tired suddenly, I closed my eyes. I would do as Peter said and try to sleep and I will not open my eyes until Peter or Judas wake me up. I took a deep breath and sighed… and I dreamed.

I once again saw Virgo, the purple silhouette, the water pot, and the green light. Virgo was wearing a black dress and she looked as if she was going to burst into tears at any moment. The purple silhouette looked at Virgo then it looked over at the light. Its eyes glowed and the light started to speak but I could not understand what it was saying.

Virgo nodded at the voice and the silhouette's entire form started to light up and glow. Finally, when the glowing stopped, Gemini was standing next to Virgo.

She looked at Virgo and then at the light. "Please give me more time." She pleaded. "Just a little longer, please."

The light once again spoke but I still could not understand what it said.

Virgo finally smiled. She looked at Gemini. "Do you agree? Do you agree Gemini?"

A gray figure came out of nowhere and revealed a vague yet rather familiar face. The person was a male geek with thick glasses. He was short and wore tight yellow jeans accompanied by black suspenders and a plain white T-shirt. He did a goofy smile and stood on the tips of his blue converse. "Do you agree, Gemini?"

Gemini put her head down in her hands. Then there was an eerie silence. The only sound was the sound of the geek man's converse shoes squeaking as he walked over to the light.

The man exhaled looking at the light. "Wow! You are really bright!" He turned his back away from the light. "Now that's better. Anyway, we will proceed as planned and not wait for ole' Gemini to give an answer?"

Gemini lifted her face. "Nathaniel, shut up before I..."

"Don't finish that sentence Gemini!" Virgo interrupted. "Look, just say yes or no? Do you agree?"

"I just need more time!"

"You said that last time." The man named Nathaniel said. He looked down and saw the water pot. He bent down and picked it up. He smelled the inside. "Smells like cinnamon and dirty water."

"Set that down." Virgo instructed.

He smelled it again. "Whose blood is this?"

Virgo snatched the water pot from him. She placed it in front of the light.

Something inaudible was being said.

Gemini inhaled and exhaled deeply. She looked at the geek. "I won't do it unless you do me a favor."

He played with his lime green wristwatch. "What favor?"

"Kill him." Gemini said hesitantly.

He bobbed his head from side to side in consideration. "No. Killing him isn't worth it."

Inaudible.

Virgo put her hand on his weak shoulders and shook him back and forth. "Just do it, kill him."

He stepped back to escape her grasp. "No. It's not worth it."

Virgo pointed at the light. "Do it, kill him."

Inaudible.

He looked at the light and squinted. "No! It's not worth it."

Gemini smiled to herself. "Then no, I don't agree."

The light grew bigger and the man shook his head.

Virgo slapped him. "Nathaniel!"

He held up his hand. "Once the great Nathaniel has made a decision, his mind cannot be changed."

"Oh, like you made the decision to try to trick Taurus into thinking you kidnapped his pride and joy? Or perhaps how you then revealed that you didn't really have his daughter?" Virgo said.

He shrugged his shoulders. "Her and those other people had some magic orb thing and they could see us. If I didn't reveal where she was, he would have killed me and then found her on his own."

Gemini looked at the light. "Am I done here?"

"Wait!" The Nathaniel man picked up the pot again. He inhaled the smell of it one last time. He pulled some of his hair out and threw it in the pot. Blue smoke came from the water pot and Nathaniel smiled. He looked as if he was staring at me. "Lancaster... Lancaster!" He laughed. "I see you."

My eyes opened and Judas was shaking my shoulder. A burst smell of eucalyptus and sweat filled my nostrils. I stood up. That smell was all he needed to wake me up.

He patted my back. "Come on buddy, we got to go."

"Where?" I asked.

An arrow wisped passed my ear. Peter came running up to me. "Sorrow about that."

"S' okay. So where are we going?"

The bow in Peter's hand disappeared. "Don't know. We should probably go to the Temple."

"How're we going to get there?" I asked.

A zombie with gray hair and a slightly torn brown business suit appeared behind Judas. He bowed at Judas and stayed silent. Judas suggested to us that we relax while the zombie go to the Temple and informed the Zodians about the city. The zombie stood motionless and was staring at me.

I glanced at him and cleared my throat. I pointed at him and Judas turned to look at him. "What?"

The zombie nodded his head then closed his hollow eyes. He buttoned his business suit then opened his eyes and bit his chapped lips. Judas just sighed and looked at Peter and me.

"Well, the Aries gem isn't available. So, we have to walk."

"Great." Peter said sarcastically. "Maybe we can board a plane and…"

All of a sudden, my eyes closed involuntarily. I saw myself standing in front of the geek. I was a Goth again. Nathaniel sat on a golden throne. His suspenders were now yellow like his teeth, his jeans gray and his T-shirt orange.

He adjusted his black top hat. "Lancaster. It is so nice to see you in person." He stood and extended his hand to me.

I shook his hand and withdrew it quickly. He laughed. "You don't have to fear me. I just want to talk to you."

"About what?"

He moved his hand and an exact replica of his throne rose behind me. "Have a seat, try it out."

I sat in the chair and rubbed my black polished nails. "What do you want to talk to me about?"

He sat on his throne and it glided across the misty floor until it settled directly in front of me. "You."

"What?" I said raising my eyebrow.

Nathaniel laughed. "Let me explain."

"Please do."

"Lancaster you have no idea who you are or what you can do. You don't know your capabilities, or your powers."

I licked the piercing on my lip from side to side. "Explain more."

"Of course. You saw me, Virgo, Gemini, and that eerie green light, remember."

"Yeah, so what? I had a dream."

"So, you don't know what Gemini was talking about?"

"No, I don't know, should I know."

"And you don't know why you're Goth?"

"No, I don't know why, what is this, a question for question game."

He stood and patted my shoulder. "Oh well. I guess later you'll find out. Until then, you can stay with me."

I stood. "No thanks. Now take me back to civilization."

"As you wish." The blackened room turned into a Middle Eastern town. People bustled passed us as if we were ghosts. The sun brightened every location in the town. The merchants could be heard over the sounds of children playing, adult men yelling at one another, and adult woman laughing as they watched the men make fools of themselves.

I turned to Nathaniel and gave a look of anger. He shrugged his shoulders and said "What? You said take you back to civilization."

"This isn't what I meant and you know it." I said in a hostile voice.

"I know, but I brought you here for a reason, Lancaster look." He pointed ahead of us and I saw a familiar face.

He had a short black and gray beard. His hair was tangled and encrusted in grime. His blue jumpsuit put him out of place. He tapped his pocket gently and walked to a merchant stand.

"Is that, is that Jebadiah?" I said.

Nathaniel nodded. "Yep, it is him. Now he has a serious plan in motion."

"What serious plan? Is it to destroy the Zodians? What is his plan?"

"Oh. I don't know. All I know is that he has a serious plan in motion."

"That's not a lot of information." I swore under my breath.

He folded his arms. "It's not my job to watch this guy and get detail information. Look, this is the pass. Now let's move on to the present, shall we."

"This sounds very familiar to me."

"Well of course it does." Nathaniel said with a big grin from ear to ear.

The environment changed to a forest. A flock of birds flew overhead to show me the red sky. The sun was setting with the accompaniment of songbirds singing as if it were their last song. A familiar redheaded figure made her way through the forest to our location. She stood in front of us and looked around.

"Mercy, what are you doing here?" I asked her.

Nathaniel tapped my shoulder. "She can't hear you. We're like ghosts."

"Oh, right."

She pulled out her cell phone and held it up. "Still no signal?" She returned her phone to her old blue jeans pocket and folded her arms. "What's the point of sending me out here?" She asked looking up.

Nathaniel adjusted his top hat. "She's out here because of her mom." He informed me.

"Her mom is making her stay out here?"

"No. Her mom banished her here for two weeks."

"What did she do to deserve banishing?"

He balanced himself on the tips of his shoes. "Something that I can't tell you about."

"I see, useless as ever in the information department."

"Good. Now, let's keep going. There is one last trip, and it's the future." The location changed again.

We were standing in front of an old shack in the middle of a swamp. Snakes slithered through our feet and I tensed my body. I saw Sofia walking up to the shack. She was in a black dress and wore a veil. Her black wedge heels clomped against the shack porch.

"What's she doing?" I asked Nathaniel.

"Just watch. Remember, this is in the future." He focused back on Sofia.

Sofia hesitated then knocked on the door. A recognizable face opened the door. Witch Greta, wearing a red robe, laughed when she laid eyes on Sofia.

Sofia shook her head and looked down. "Help me."

"What was that dear, speak up, I can't hear you. Did you say something?" She said in a taunting voice.

Sofia got down on her knees and started to cry. "I killed him."

Witch Greta patted her back. "Good, that's a good girl."

"No, it's not. I… He was a good guy."

"Then why is he dead? If he was so good why did you kill him?"

"Please, bring him back." Sofia begged.

Witch Greta gazed her black eyes behind us. "The sun rises in a few minutes child. You should get going."

"Please!" Sofia stood. "Bring him back to me!"

"No." Witch Greta turned her back. "And if you kill me, you know what will happen. So, don't even think about it."

Sofia was enraged and a silhouette covered her body. "It's worth it."

In the blink of an eye with a bright explosion Witch Greta was gone. The silhouette went away and Sofia smiled. "May your twisted mangled soul be unrest in..." She stopped when she heard a scream.

The three of us turned simultaneously and saw it was Judas. His eyes were blue and his hair was blonde. If it wasn't for his voice, I wouldn't have recognized him.

He laughed. "I knew screaming would get your attention. Come on, your dad is looking for you."

I blinked and Nathaniel and I were back in the middle of nowhere. The thrones reappeared and he sat down. He motioned me to sit on the throne in front of him.

I sat down and frowned as I thought about the trip through time. "What's Jebadiah's plan? What did Mercy do to get banished for two weeks? Who did Sofia kill and why? How is Judas still alive without the Aries Gem?"

Nathaniel took a deep breath. "I don't know. Virgo would kill me if I told you anyway. But just remember, the future can be changed."

"How can I change the future? How can I change the future?" Everything looked really misty and hazy all of a sudden.

"Whoops! Looks like we're out of time! I got to go, bye Lancaster!"

"Wait! Wait, don't go yet, wait!" My eyes closed involuntarily and I felt as if I was falling.

When my eyes opened, I saw that Peter had me across his broad shoulders carrying me. I cleared my throat and he stopped walking.

He set me down and sighed. "You okay?"

"Yeah, am okay. Why?"

"You were out for three days. I thought you were dead."

"Really, three days?"

Judas came running up behind us. "Peter! Peter, I found…" He stopped and stared at me. "Lancaster? I thought you died."

"I know I know. What did I miss?"

"Look around you."

I did as Judas said. We were standing on a sidewalk next to a very busy street. The sound of car horns and people talking on cellphones almost distracted me from the mixed smell of sewage and hot dogs.

I shrugged my shoulders. "Where are we? Is this Kansas?"

"No, it's New York City." Someone hit me in the back of the head.

I turned around to find Sofia. "Uh… hi, hello."

She rolled her eyes. "What happened to you?"

"The question is how did we get to New York City?"

"Answer my question first. How did we get to New York city?"

Peter clapped his hands. "Enough, Sofia used the silhouettes to get us here."

"Why won't you answer my question, Lancaster?" Sofia folded her arms frowning at me.

"Because we don't know the answer." Judas said. He fixed his orange ski hat.

"Lancaster, the answer now. What happened to you?"

"I honestly don't know. I just blacked out, okay." I lied.

Sofia hit my head again. "Stop lying."

"Okay, okay." I rubbed my head. "I closed my eyes and saw Mercy cast a spell on me." I said involuntarily. In fact, I didn't even realize I said that until after Sofia said something to me.

"Of course." Sofia shook her head.

"Maybe she had a good reason for doing the spell." Peter said.

"Or not." Judas took off his sun glasses. "Maybe she's planning something against us."

"Or maybe the plan is already in motion." Peter said wiping the side of his face.

"You could be right." Sofia said quietly.

"Or maybe, I was just dreaming."

"You were asleep for three days." Sofia said shaking my shoulders. "This has to be Mercy's doing."

"Or maybe just maybe, I was just dreaming." I suggested again.

Judas shook his head. "She's already controlling his mind! We have to save him before it's too late!"

People started to gather around and stared at Judas and his ghoulish looks. They whispered to each other and listened intently.

Judas pounded his fist against his hand and didn't even notice the people. "She has to be stopped before she gets us all! Maybe this is all Virgo's plan! Yes! This is all Virgo's doing! Virgo will kill us if we don't…"

Sofia ran and covered his mouth. She looked at the people. "Don't you people have jobs or somewhere to be?" They all walked away saying Virgo's name over and over again.

Sofia looked down at Judas. "How could you say a Zodian's name like that? Now the entire city will be talking about her. Then the four of us will be in big trouble."

She moved her hand from his mouth. Judas licked his lips and smiled with a nod of his shoulders.

"Aren't you even a little worried?" She asked him.

"No, I am really not worried. I'm Judas, the dead." He said so cavalierly.

"Well we're not dead and we would like to keep it that way." Peter reminded him. "Let's find a place to stay for the night." Peter started walking.

Sofia and Judas followed behind him. I looked around and shook my head and went into deep thought. Sometime in the future Sofia would murder someone and then ask Witch Greta for help. Judas wouldn't need the Aries Gem anymore and I didn't know why. Although Nathaniel told me that the future could be changed, but he didn't tell me how to change it. By the time I finished thinking about all these things, the others were gone. And once more I was left alone.

I stomped my foot. "Great, just great. I am alone again." I started walking forward.

As I walked the warm daytime air grew colder with every step I took. The New Yorkers all stopped as I walked pass them. They all looked afraid and I didn't know why. I would look at them and they would turn their heads from me or run. I exhaled and it started to snow. I rubbed my uncovered arms as the ground filled with snow. Everyone seemed to stop looking at me as they took notice to the snow. They all started talking about how it can snow in the middle of spring. I was curious about that myself.

It was an extreme change in temperature. I exhaled again and my bones grew very numb. I only felt that way one other time. It was when I was crossing the Strait of Gibraltar. The temperature kept dropping and my skin started to turn blue and my body was nearly frozen. My lips froze together and I stopped walking. I stood in front of a newsstand and looked at the papers.

The man stared at me but I didn't stare back. I pointed at a newspaper and he handed it to me. "N-n-no charge." He said through chattering partly frozen teeth.

I took the newspaper and looked at the front page. The title read, 'City of Seattle in Chaos.' My right eye froze shut. I read on, 'Seattle is now literally sleepless. Six military helicopters flew over the city, but only two returns. The survivors say that the people acted as zombies. Military soldiers are now being sent in to contain and examine the people. Is this the sign of Armageddon or the sign of not enough coffee?'

I sighed. Soon Seattle wouldn't be the only city sleepless. I slowly and painfully opened my right eye back. When it opened, I folded the newspaper and kept walking. Every time my feet hit the ground I grunted. I feel much worse now than I did when I was crossing the Strait of Gibraltar. I fell to the ground and the newspaper rolled out of my hand frozen. My knees felt as if they were broken and my legs felt like ice sickles. The snow fell harder. My hands stuck to the snow-covered ground. When saliva would drip from my mouth it would immediately turn into ice and fall off.

I felt weak and I could feel the touch of Aries. I saw him as a spirit standing before me. He stretched out his hand and I turned my head away from him.

"You cannot escape death." He told me.

I tried to stand but my legs and feet were paralyzed. I looked at him. "Uncle Aries, please save me."

He sighed and his figure went from a spirit to a person. "I have already helped you twice now."

"Give me one last chance. After that, you can take me."

"Lancaster…"

"Please!" I yelled painfully. "There's so much people haven't told me about myself. I don't want to die before knowing more about myself. I need to live."

"I can tell you everything you want to know when you come with me."

"Then it'll be too late, please help me."

He got on his knees. "Okay, this is the last time; I will not help you again. I am your uncle but I am also Aries, the Zodian god of Death. I cannot continue to let your soul live."

"Thank you, thank you, thank you."

"You are welcome."

"Wait?"

"Now what?"

"What's going on with New York City and this weather?" I asked.

With hesitation he said "The unnatural weather is being caused by a sorcerer or sorceress. Perhaps it is the person trying to find the weaknesses of the Zodians."

"Maybe."

He stood. "The next time you die, your soul must stay in The After Life."

"I understand, and it will."

"Good bye."

"Bye." A bright light blinded me and I was lying in front of a hotdog cart.

The snow stopped falling but there was a big accumulation of snow on the ground. I stood up and wiped the snow off of my pants. I looked and saw other people rising to their feet. Some weren't moving. The man at the hotdog cart lay motionless. I fixed myself a hotdog and left him five dollars that I found buried in the snow. "Keep the change."

I crossed the street by jumping over wrecked cars and avoiding metal pieces. I caught sight of an orange ski hat in the snow. I dropped the hotdog and ran to the hat. There was no head under it. A pair of sun glasses lay beside the hat.

I looked around. "Judas?" I picked up the hat and sun glasses and walked around the corner. People were panicking and calling the police, weather station, firefighters, and the Army. I walked up to a lady who was kneeling in the snow and crying above a little boy. She was trying her best to explain to the operator what had happened. I got on my knees and patted her shoulder. "Um... are you okay?"

She turned to me and dropped the phone. She pointed down at the little boy. "He's dead!" She started to cry on my shoulder.

I looked down at her. "Um, it's okay."

"No, it's not!" She sobbed.

"Look, I'm sure he's in a better place. I mean maybe he has a choice between two places, a paradise or a living nightmare." I said from experience.

She lifted her face from my shoulder. "What's your religion?"

"Zodianism, I guess."

"Lancaster!" A familiar voice said.

I looked up. "Judas?"

He came running up to me. "Dude! I've been looking for you everywhere." He looked at the lady.

The woman stood up and stepped away from him. "What are you?"

Ignoring the question from the lady, Judas looked down at the boy. "Your son?"

She nodded and sobbed again. Judas knelt down with his eyes closed and put his hand on the boy's forehead. The boy's eyes twitched and then opened. The boy jumped up when he saw Judas. He quickly looked at his mom. "Mommy!" He jumped in her arms.

The woman held her son tight as she looked at Judas. "What did you do to him?!"

"I just brought him back to life for you."

She looked at him then me over and over again. "What kind of magic is this? And thank you."

I smiled. "It's a part of our religion."

With her son in her arms the woman ran off.

Judas looked down and picked up the phone. His crimson eyes widened. He showed me the phone and I saw that the operator was still on the line.

Do you think the person heard us? I mouthed to him.

He shrugged his shoulders and hung up the phone. "If they did hear us then we better change our names."

I handed him his hat and sun glasses. "Where is Sofia and Peter?"

"Don't know." He said putting on his accessories. "I was walking behind them when I felt something hit my head. I looked up and saw it was snow. I looked at the people around me and saw that it wasn't just snow. Peter and Sofia both fell. When I walked over to them…" He paused. "…I saw they were dead…"

My eyes widened and my heart tightened. "You didn't save them?!"

"I would've but Aries blocked my powers. He told me that he wouldn't let me save them." He sniffed and cleared his throat. "I just saved that little boy because I wanted to see if the Gem's powers came back."

I sighed. "The Zodians can deactivate their Gems' powers?"

"Yes."

"Then why don't they all do that? It saves us time and doesn't threaten humanity."

"I'm not them, so I don't know why not. Look, we have to save Sofia and Peter. If Taurus finds whoever killed his daughter, the world will not exist anymore. And if Sagittarius finds whoever killed Peter, he'll unleash his other side."

"His other side? What does that mean?"

"Sagittarius may appear to be kind and gentle, but on the inside, he has a totally different personality. Peter was always like a son to him. When he finds who did this, he will gladly help Taurus destroy the earth."

"Then let's try and bring them back. Fast."

He stretched out his arms. "Hold on to my arm."

I did as he said without hesitation.

"Close your eyes and don't open them until I tell you to."

"Why?"

"Because... we're going to The After Life to get Sofia and Peter."

I didn't bother telling him about my last encounter with my uncle. Aries said that if I die, I would have to stay there. He never said that if I go save my friends from him, I would forever dwell there. Loophole. I closed my eyes and immediately felt hands.

They tampered with my ears and I felt one graze my heart. I heard laughter and screaming, but mostly laughter. The hands left me and I got goose bumps when I heard voices calling my name incessantly. They called me in a whisper and laughed loudly. The hairs on the back of my neck stood on end when I heard Judas say, "Okay. You can open your eyes."

I opened one eye and looked around. I opened my other eye and saw that I was in an office with red carpeting, eggplant walls, with a leather couch next to a long window with curtains. Two leather chairs sat uneven in front of a cherry wood desk with papers neatly piled, a pencil cup, a black laptop, and a tray full of papers with people's names and all of their information. The word DECEASED was stamped on the papers.

Judas sighed and took a seat. "Sit down."

I sat down and straightened my seat until it was even. "Where are we?"

"We are in Aries' office."

I turned and looked at the blue door. "Where is he?"

He crossed his legs. "Don't know. All I know is that he's coming in here sooner or later."

"Why don't we just go find him?"

He took off his hat and sun glasses and set them in his lap. "He doesn't like or want me to just show up in The After Life. Why? I don't know. He just doesn't."

"So, we'll wait here for him because when he comes that means he might not be busy. So, he can't avoid us."

"Okay, I understand now"

"Yeah, now you're getting it."

I sat back in the chair and tried to relax. "Where is this office located?"

"Above the ground." Judas said smiling ghoulishly.

"So, it's floating in mid-air?"

"Yep. It's not dangerously close to the pathway, but it is close enough and centered enough for him to see everything that's happening here."

I sighed. "Do you think he'll give Sofia and Peter back?"

"Don't know. It probably depends on his mood."

The door flew open and a man dressed in green shorts and a red shirt stepped him. When he saw us, he quickly ripped his earphones from his ears. He took off his barely visible sweaty white sweatband and dragged his black athletic shoes to the chair behind the desk. He set his iPod and earphones on the desk and set his sweatband in the tray. He shook his white hair. "Why are you here?" He asked as if he already knew the answer.

"To get our friends back." Judas said.

He sat back in his chair until the light no longer revealed his face. In the dark his face looked the same as a skeleton's. "I can't do that."

"You can, you just won't." I said sternly.

He pointed at me. "Right. Listen, Peter and Sofia's souls are mine. They are somewhat happy and I will not let them leave here."

"Come on Aries!" Judas yelled. "Taurus won't stand for his daughter being here and Sagittarius will blow when he finds out what happened to Peter."

Aries sat forward. "Those two are welcome to try to get them back."

"But not us, we can't try and get them back?" I said.

"Exactly. Now leave and don't return unless you die."

Judas stood up angrily. "I'm not leaving here without them." He said banging on the desk.

Aries began flipping through the papers in the tray until he found the two, he wanted. He handed them to Judas.

Judas sat down and we looked at the papers:

Name: Samantha Sofia
Date of birth: January 1, 1998
Hair color: brown
Eye color: green, changed to purple
Date of death: April 7, 2012
Cause of death: unusual weather caused by magic

Name: Peter Arcadian O'Hara
Date of birth: March 4, 1990
Hair color: black
Eye color: black
Date of death: April 7, 2012
Cause of death: unusual weather caused by magic

I sat back and closed my eyes. "Uncle Aries, please give them back."

"Uncle?" Judas asked.

My eyes shot open and Aries was looking down. I cleared my throat. "I didn't say uncle."

Judas turned and looked at me. "Yes, you did."

I gulped. "No, I didn't."

"Yes, you did."

Aries stood and took the papers from Judas. "Both of you get out."

"Not without Peter and Sofia." Judas said slowly.

"Out."

"I got an Idea." I said. "If you release them... you can have my soul."

Aries sat back down. "If you do that, only one can leave." He looked at Judas.

Judas looked down. "Um..."

"You felt death once." Aries said smiling. "Why not feel it once more?"

Judas looked up. "I know your game. I won't play it again." He said in a low voice. He put his hat and sun glasses on and walked to the door.

I turned around and looked at him. "Judas. What game?"

"Ask your uncle." The door opened and closed making me feel strange inside.

I looked at Aries. "Sorry for telling Judas that you're my uncle."

"You should've never come here."

"You should've released my friends sooner."

"You should've stayed here in the first place."

"You should've not let me go."

"You should've not asked me to save you."

"You should've not listened to a child."

"You should've..." He sighed. "Which friend do you want to save?"

I stood up. "What game was Judas talking about?"

He took the rest of the papers out of the tray and started scanning threw them. "I don't know."

"Don't lie, uncle."

"Why would I play games?"

"To trick people into dying. It keeps this place full and you happy knowing that your work continues." I said in shock of myself.

He glanced up at me. "You are certainly Aquarius's son."

"I'm proud of it."

"Of course, you are." He stood up and walked to the window. "Exit the door and you will be on earth again."

"I'm not leaving until you give me both of my friends back."

"Have it your way."

The door flew open and two zombies dressed in camouflage uniforms entered. They each grabbed one of my arms.

Aries turned his head slightly. "So long nephew."

The two zombies dragged me to the door. I tried to move but I couldn't. "I'll get them back!"

"No, you won't."

The two threw me out the room and I started falling and feeling fire. I closed my eyes and felt hands touching me and heard the laughter again. The falling stopped and I opened my eyes slowly and saw Judas standing over me. We were back in New York.

He helped me up and slapped the back of my head. We started to walk when he said "You played his game."

"What game did I play?" I asked as we stepped over dead bodies and crying people. We were still in a chaotic New York City.

"Aries' game." Judas said.

"More details please, what game?"

"Why didn't you ask your uncle for details about his game?"

"I did and he wouldn't tell me."

"It's because you can't keep a secret. So, I won't tell you."

"Just tell me what game you are talking about?"

"Look, you're not going to tell anyone… right? Can you keep a secret or not? He looked down.

"I won't tell. But the Elders are going to find out eventually anyway, whatever it is."

"And what if they don't find out?" He looked at me and grinned. "What do you think nephew of Aries?"

"Stop." I said in a loud irritated voice.

"Why should I stop, nephew of Aries? Do you not like the fact that…"?

"No, I mean stop and look!" I stuck my arm out in front of him.

We both looked and saw Virgo. She was standing with her back up against a display window. Next to her on the ground sat Nathaniel.

Judas eyes squinted curiously looking. "Who's that guy with her?"

"Come on." I said ignoring his question. We both slowly walked over to them.

Virgo laughed when she caught sight of us. "Have you two come to give me my Gem?"

"No." I said.

"Then leave my presence at once!"

"We need you to persuade Aries to…"

"To what? Give the muscular boy and Taurus' daughter back." Virgo said interrupting Judas.

"How'd you know?" He asked taking off his sun glasses.

She smiled. "All of the Elders know. Taurus and Sagittarius are on their way to talk to Aries right now."

"Great!" I said smiling. "So, Peter and Sofia are going to be okay." I said with a burst of happiness.

"I wouldn't count on it." Nathaniel said standing up. He looked at Judas's eyes. "You, you have the Aries Gem."

"Yeah. So?"

"So, why don't you bring the two back?"

"Aries deactivated the Gem when I tried to bring them back to life."

"Makes sense." Nathaniel said. "Virgo, I believe you have a message for Mr. Lancaster."

Virgo sighed and rolled her eyes. "Libra has requested your presence."

"Libra? He has requested my presence, why?"

"Don't know don't care. Let's go." A gray cloud surrounded us. "Don't move or you'll die."

"Well I guess that applies to you dude" Judas said with a grin.

"Thanks for the warning." I said holding perfectly still looking at Judas then looking at the cloud as it thickens around us. The cloud turned into mist and rolled away revealing the throne room in the Temple. The throne room was vacant except for Cancer. He was sitting on his brain shaped throne. He tapped his iPod then set it down as he opened a pizza box.

Virgo rolled her eyes. "Cancer. Cancer. Cancer!" When he didn't respond she grunted. Cancer chewed his pizza as he looked down at a comic book. He was completely oblivious that we were staring at him. She blocked his lighting then slapped his forehead. "Cancer!"

"Ow!" He dropped the slice of pizza and the food in his mouth. "Why'd ya do that?!"

"To get your attention."

He closed the comic book and picked up the falling pizza slice and put on top of the pizza box. He then picked up the chewed food with a napkin. "Well you could've tapped my shoulder or something."

"Where's Libra?"

He stood up and finally saw the rest of us. "What's Nathaniel doing here?"

Half shyly, Nathaniel waved at him and said nothing.

So, Cancer said "You just following Virgo around."

Virgo snapped her fingers in front of Cancer's face. "Focus. Where's Libra?"

Cancer sat back. "He was here then he left. He told me to relax so I ordered a pizza and bought myself a comic book to read."

"Where did you order the pizza and buy a comic from?" I asked.

He smiled at me. "If I told you, you wouldn't believe me."

Virgo sighed. "So, you don't know where Libra is."

"No. He didn't tell me where he was going."

"Where does he usually go to?" Judas asked.

Virgo sat on her throne and crossed her legs. "Everywhere. He's the Zodian god of Balance. He has to make sure everything is in balance."

Nathaniel nodded. "Space."

"Space?" I repeated.

"Yeah." He said confidently. "In space he can see the earth…"

"Which means he can see everything." I interrupted Nathaniel, finishing his sentence.

Virgo looked up. "I am not going into space."

"You don't have to go." Nathaniel told her. "Lancaster does." He said patting my back.

"Me? Space."

"Yes you. Libra wants to speak to you."

"Right." I said holding in my fear. "But uh… there's uh… there's no way I can get into space so…"

"Yes, there is." Virgo walked to me and pushed me to a wall. "Go through it."

"Oh no! I remember the last time I went through one of these walls."

"This is the right one. I promise."

"I should go with him." Judas suggested.

"No!" Nathaniel said pushing him back. "I mean… he wants to talk to Lancaster only."

Judas raised his left white eyebrow at Nathaniel. "Fine."

"Great." Virgo said pushing me closer to the wall. "Now go."

"Wait!" Cancer ran over to me. "Let me go with him."

"Why?"

"Just let me go with him." He pointed behind him to tell Virgo to leave. She rolled her eyes and walked back over to her throne.

"Why do you want to come with me?" I asked him.

He patted my back and smiled. "Ready?"

"No, but yeah."

He pushed me and I heard him laugh as he jumped in behind me going through the wall. Instead of seeing equations, this time I saw bright lights and Cancer screaming his head off. "The lights are so bright! So bright!"

I squinted and laughed. The lights went away and I saw tiny lights and darkness. "Can't… breath!" I yelled in a whisper.

Cancer floated in front of me moving his hands in a circle and touched my shoulder. "Better right? I put an invisible shield around you so you can breathe."

"Thanks." I started to look around and saw all the planets. It was space.

They all were align and started moving to the right. In a matter of minutes, the planets switched orders. Now the order was: Pluto, Neptune, Uranus, Saturn, Jupiter, Mars, Earth, Venus, and Mercury.

My eyes widened. "Did you see that?!" I said excitedly.

Cancer nodded. "I swear I didn't do that. Maybe I could if I really wanted to, but I didn't do that!"

I tapped his shoulder. "Look!" The sun started to move pass the planets.

"What's going on?!"

"The balance is changing." A voice said.

"Oh, my Zodiac! I'm hearing voices now!" Cancer said as he grabbed his face. "What does this mean?! Am I going crazy?!"

"No Cancer, it's just Libra." I said slowly looking at him.

He turned around and smiled. "Oh, thank goodness! For a minute there, I thought…well you know."

Libra floated to us. "There is too much sorcery going on in the earth and the universe is out of balance. One person is somehow harvesting all of the power and using it to slowly end the earth. You must go back to the beginning of magic in the earth and find that person."

Cancer began to whimper. "Will I die too if the earth ends?!"

Libra shook his head. "Cancer you are immortal, get a grip on yourself."

"Oh right, good, thanks for the reminder! You scared me for a moment… just a moment."

"Lancaster, your world is in danger and you must save it." Libra said sadly.

"And I have to save it because…Sofia and Peter are dead and it's up to me now, right? Well what about Judas? Why can't he save it?" I asked Libra.

"Aries will soon take his Gem away from Judas, he has no power."

"How soon will Aries take it away; we may have time for Judas to save the world?"

"No, there is no time, it must be you. This is your journey; it is your true destiny."

"How can I change the balance of the earth by myself?"

"I will send you to the first days of magic." Libra's eyes started to glow through his armor.

"When will you send me?"

"Now." Said Libra.

"What, you mean now as in right now?"

"Bye Lancaster!" Cancer said quickly.

"Wait! I need to pack my things first or something, am not ready!" I yelled.

"When you get there, you will soon know what to do." Libra said.

A bright light surrounded me. "Wait, wait please wait. Get where, exactly where am I going, where is this beginning of magic?!"

"Relax and do what you must to save humanity."

"But am not ready, I need…" The light grew brighter. "I'll need help!"

"You will get it."

"Just calm down Lancaster." Cancer said. "You can save the world, no pressure, you can do it. You can save the world."

The light blinded me and Cancer's last words echoed in my ears, "You can save the world."

The Making of a King

"Arthur. Arthur. Arthur wake up."

My eyes peeled open very slowly to a strange voice. I rubbed my eyes as I noticed that I was lying on matted straw. I lifted my head and looked around. I didn't recognize anything; I was in a stone house. I sat up and immediately found myself face to face with a bearded man.

My eyes widened and the man smiled. "Did you slumber peacefully last night?" His accent made him seem British. His brown attire gave him the persona of a peasant.

I stood up and backed away from him.

"Arthur? Are you alright?" The man asked with concern in his eyes.

"Arthur? Who is Arthur?" I asked myself softly while looking around.

The bearded man ran his hand threw my much longer hair. "Did something strike your head?"

"Arthur, Ector?" A British voiced woman slowly entered the room. "I need you two to go to the market and bring meat." She wiped her damp hands on her pink renaissance dress.

"Yes dear." The man said. "Come Arthur." He said placing his hand on my shoulder.

I shrugged his hand off my shoulder. "Arthur?"

The woman gave me the same confused look as the man. "Have you forgotten your own name?"

I looked down. Why are they calling me Arthur? I asked myself. I thought about it until the man playfully slapped my shoulder and startled me.

"Come Arthur. Let us find meat at the market." He then turned and left.

I followed him with extreme caution. When I left out of the stone house, I said one word, "Whoa."

I saw more stone houses. In the distance my ears heard music that you would hear in a king's court. I saw children playing with sticks while teenage boys brawled amongst each other and teenage girls rooting for them. Trees surrounded me and they were accompanied by tiny animals finding food on their own.

I looked to my right and saw a teenage boy with a hoe tending to the ground around the house.

"Kay." The man called. "Come. Your mother requests that we bring meat."

The teenage boy wiped his face with the back of his filthy hand. He shook his head to no one in particular. "Yes father." He didn't have the accent like the man or the woman. He did have an accent, but one that sounded Australian.

He walked to me and playfully slapped my shoulder. "Good day brother."

"Brother?" I asked to ensure I heard him correctly.

He brushed the dirt off his clothes. "Yes. I am your brother." He said slowly. "Are you alright?"

"Yeah." I said quickly. "So, are we going to the market or not?" I asked hastily.

"Yes." The man started walking.

The boy called Kay walked behind him. I followed them like a mouse. Arthur? Ector? Kay? Where am I? I asked myself. At that moment, I remembered what Libra told me. He would send me back to the place where magic first started. Then I remembered I have to save humanity by going to a place where some magical person would be. When I would get to that place,

I would have to do something to stop the person from destroying the earth. I then realized that I had forgotten to ask Libra a very important question: How do I find the person and exactly who am I supposed to stop?! I stopped thinking when I bumped into the boy named Kay. He turned and looked at me. "Are you sure you are okay?" He asked.

"Uh… yeah… I'm fine." I stammered.

The man stood between us at that moment. He handed me a bag and the boy a bag. "Spend wisely. I'll find you when I'm done." He left the two of us standing in silence.

Kay smiled at the bag. "At last." He said as he ran off.

I slowly opened the bag and saw copper and silver coins. I looked at them closely. "These aren't pennies or quarters or any other form of change like that."

I looked up and saw people playing instruments such as flutes and fiddles. As the people played others were buying various items from merchant stands. More little boys ran around with sticks and little girls played with rag dolls. I heard women laughing and saw Kay laughing right with them.

I looked in the bag again. I looked to find a president but there wasn't one. Instead I saw 45 on the front of the silver pieces and 20 on the front of the copper pieces. On the back of the coins were weird symbols.

I finally started walking. I passed by merchants who were telling me to stop by them and buy all kinds of things. I ignored all of them except one. I only stopped because I saw he had a mirror. I stood close to it and finally saw myself. My hair was still brown only now it touched my shoulder. I was wearing red pants made out of cloth and a gray shirt along with blue shoes. "What the…?"

"Can I help you boy?" The merchant asked me interrupting my thought process. His voice was slimy.

I snapped my head toward him. "Yes. Where am I?"

The man laughed but stopped when he saw I was being serious. "You're in Grassland."

"Grassland?" I asked.

The man held up his index finger as he rummaged through the clutter on his table. He found a map. "Look." He said as he rolled it out on the table.

The map showed three colors: crimson, cerulean, and emerald. The emerald part was the largest, then cerulean and finally crimson. Emerald was on top and had cerulean right beside it. Crimson was beneath the emerald and separated by what looked to be a good bit of ocean. On the emerald part in permanent marker was written GRASSLAND. On the cerulean was written MOUNTAIN. On the crimson was written DESERT.

The man folded the map back and pulled out a book. He placed the map in the front of the book and handed it to me. "Take it… for free."

I took the book from him and smiled. "Thank you."

The man nodded.

I stopped two merchant stands down when I saw a book. A book titled The Gift of Magic. I picked up the book and opened it. I coughed when the dust flew in my face off the book. Maybe the book would help me find or do whatever I was supposed to find or do.

"It's yours for the right price." The merchant said rubbing his fingers together.

"How much is the book?" I said setting the thick book back down.

"Fifty."

"Fifty?" I had a sneaking feeling about the merchant but I paid him anyway. I gave him one silver coin and one copper coin and he handed me a coin that almost felt wooden.

"Enjoy." He said after a hearty laugh.

I picked the book back up. "Thanks." I walked away with my face in the book. The book was old and smelled like Witch Greta's shack.

I eventually found a merchant stand that had a messenger bag. I paid 40 cents or dollars or whatever for it and placed the books in the bag. I strapped the bag around me and went on my way.

I roamed around until I found Kay. He was gazing lively at weapons. He held a regular sword in his hand. He set it down and placed a bronze helmet on his head.

I walked up behind him and tapped his shoulder. "Kay?"

He turned around quickly and relaxed when he saw it was me. He removed the helmet. "What?"

"Are you really going to buy a sword and helmet?" I asked.

"Perhaps I will." He turned to the merchant. "What's the price for the helmet and sword?"

The man scratched his ear. "The sword is 45 and the helmet is 100."

Kay sighed. "Can you lower the helmets price?"

The man merchant shook his head. "Sorry."

"Can I at least get a sheath for the sword for free?"

The man thought for a moment. "Yes."

Kay turned to me. "Should I buy the sword?" He asked me.

I shrugged my shoulders. "Will you use it?"

Kay turned back to the man and opened the bag the man called Ector gave him. He placed a silver coin on the table and picked up the sword. The man handed Kay a sheath for the sword. Kay walked away without a show of gratitude. He placed the sword in the sheath and smiled. I followed behind him shortly. "How much money do you have?" Kay asked me.

I walked up beside him and opened the little bag the man called Ector gave me. He stopped walking and looked inside my bag. "You still have quite a few coins left. Did you spend your money on the bag only?"

"No." I pulled the books from the bag.

He glanced at the map book but stared at the magic book. He took the magic book from me. "You bought a book of magic?"

I took it back from him and put it and the other book back in the bag. "Yeah."

"Why?" Kay asked in a low voice.

"I just wanted it." I lied. There was no way I could tell him the real reason why I got the book. I shouldn't have even showed him the book.

The man named Ector walked up to us. "Alright let us return home." He had a dead pig thrown across his shoulder. In his free hand he held a bag full of vegetables and a bag full of fruits.

The three of us walked back to the stone house to see the woman standing in the doorway. She and the man went inside the house. Kay set the sword on the ground, picked up the hoe, and started working again.

I needed to start looking at the books as soon as possible. I walked to the back of the house and sat down with my back against the house's smooth wall. A brown horse and a white horse were both caged inside a wooden fence. The brown horse walked around the area as the white horse lay down asleep. I opened the book with the map in it. I read about each of the three countries. Basically, I was still on earth but not in America. From what I read I could see that the Desert was basically like Australia.

The book said that Desert was the worse place to live. Desert was sunny and hot. That meant no crops grew. There were only sand and wild animals that would be hunted for food. The people that lived there were often referred to as Cannibals since they only ate meat. The houses were mud huts and big enough to house four people, however rather uncomfortably. It never rained and there were never any clouds. The only water source was a tiny pond directly in the middle of Desert. That meant any time someone was in the mood for a glass of water they would have to make a two-day journey for water. The main occupation of the people was hunting. The book said that it was the smallest country out of the three.

Mountain was the complete opposite. Mountain was just that, mountains. It was a knock off of Canada. Mountain was home of what were called the Mountaineers. Mountain was only inhabited by men. There was never a woman that stepped foot on Mountaineer territory. It always snowed in Mountain so no crops grew there either. The people hunted too but the main occupation was engineering. All of the houses were built into mountains. There was only one avalanche reported and it killed 4,807 people. This made a really big dent in the population. Mountain was the second largest country.

Grassland was the most populated and largest country. It was the ideal place to live. The crops grew exceptionally and it always rained at the right time. The main occupation was tied between mercantilism and farming. The houses were either made of stone or brick (the poor had stone, the rich had brick). I'm not too sure which country Grassland was supposed to be like, but I guess Britain because of the accents.

I put the map book back in the bag and pulled out the spell book. I didn't really read it like I read the other book. I just glanced through it.

Page nine of the book was full of instruction on how to levitate objects. Page fifteen showed how to control nature. Page twenty-one talked all about how to raise the dead. Page thirty-three had a picture of a green light and a… watering pot! Just like what I saw before. Holy Zodiac!

The page read: The Holy Illuminati holds all magical powers of all spell bound humans and beings. In the pot lies the blood of a force none know of. It is said that if any partake of the blood, they will have incredible power. In order to have this power, the wielder must chant…

"Arthur?"

I stood quickly when I saw the familiar woman stand in front of me. "Ma'am?" I answered.

"What are you looking at?" She asked.

I put the book back in the bag as fast as I could. "Nothing."

"Well, help Kay with his farming while your father and I start preparing the meal."

I nodded and ran to Kay. He stopped working when he saw me. "Yes brother?" He asked.

"Um… that woman…uh… I mean… mom wants me to help you with your farming." I assumed she was his… our mother.

He laughed. "I don't need your help. I can do this on my own… just like always."

"Tell mom you don't need help; she wants me to help you." I said with uncertainty in my tone.

He stuck the tool in the ground and rested himself on it. "No, I will not tell her that." He made his way to the house, looking back he said "Help me by finishing my work for me." He walked in the house but not without taking his newly purchased weapon with him.

I threw my bag on the ground and pulled the hoe from the ground. "What am I supposed to do with this thing?"

I started raking the ground continuously. I did that over and over again. It felt like I was doing that for hours but I wasn't sure because I didn't have a watch. In fact, the book said that Grassland, like Desert, lacked electricity. Only Mountains had electricity, lucky them.

My muscles ached and I was sweating everywhere. I dropped the tool and fell on my knees. "Why is working so hard?" While I was attempting to check my pulse a pair of brown shoes came into my sight. "Arthur?" Ector showed his strength by lifting me to my feet. He closely examined me.

"We wanted you to help Kay not do his job completely. Are you alright?"

I picked up my bag. "I'm tired and sore, but fine."

"Good. Come on inside, the food is ready."

After we ate, Kay left to finish his work on his own and Ector and his wife left to go speak to neighbors briefly. I went back to the room I woke up in.

I sat down on the pile of straw and opened the magic book to the last page I was on. The other book gave me helpful information but it didn't tell me what century or what year I was in. All I know is that it had to be the future because the book had the water pot with my blood in it. Unless it was someone else's blood.

I needed a place with a wide variety of books. I needed a library. Since Grassland was the most prominent country it had to have a library. I just needed to find it.

I stood up and walked outside the house. Kay stopped his work and laughed when he saw me holding the book. "Where are you going with that?"

Not answering, I put the book in my bag and walked to the back of the hut. I opened the fence around the horses and walked to the brown horse which stood still when it saw me. I patted its head and it reared back and I told him to relax. The horse did as I said. I gently and slowly lifted myself up on the horse. I rode a horse before when I was 7, but it wasn't really a horse… it was just a pony. The pony ended up causing me to break my leg and I hadn't ridden a horse since.

I was sure that this horse was different. In a somber voice I said "Yaw!" The horse started off fast but slowed down to a trot.

Kay stopped working when he saw me ride by. "Arthur, you know father doesn't like you riding the horses."

"Tell dad. I'll pay the price." I said without caring. He wasn't my real dad anyway.

He shook his head. "Father is going to be angry."

Before I could respond Ector and his wife darted over. Ector halted when he saw me on the horse. He shook his head at me and then gathered his thoughts back in focus. The horse and I stood still. He placed his hands-on Kay's shoulders. "Kay! I have splendid news!"

Kay grinned ear to ear. "Do tell father."

"A sword has been found placed in a stone."

"And?" Kay asked as his grin started to wither away.

"Whosoever pulls the sword from the stone shall be the new king of Grassland." Ector said slowly.

"Where is the sword now?" Kay asked rapidly.

"The sword has been placed in the center of the castles jousting arena." Ector replied.

Kay's eyes widened with excitement. "I will try… I will get the sword out of the stone. I will go get my armor."

"Excellent!" The woman said.

Kay ran in the house without another word.

I jumped down from the horse and had a gloom expression. Ector noticed. "Arthur, what is wrong?"

"Nothing." I said quickly.

The woman hugged me. "Arthur dear, it is not that we believe you can't pull the sword from the stone."

"Then what? Why wasn't I asked too?" I asked sternly.

The man cleared his throat. "Kay is strong and you are…"

"And I'm not. Yeah I understand." I was seriously hurt. I mean it was just like the time I tried out for Garamond's high school football team but I was turned down because I wasn't strong, didn't have enough energy, and to small. So, what if I looked like a bobble head when I wore the football helmet.

"Arthur…" The woman suddenly stopped talking and started to stare with pride.

Kay walked out the stone house like a superhero would. He was now wearing knight's armor and a black cape. With his sword at his side he placed himself up on the horse. He didn't speak he just rode off.

Ector ran back behind the house. I watched him as he sat himself up on the other horse. He rode up to my mother and me. "I have to watch Kay pull the sword from the stone."

The woman smiled and entered the house. I looked at Ector. "Does this mean I stay here?"

Ector didn't say a word. His horse galloped off.

I kicked the ground and grunted. I felt left out just like in Seattle when everyone was leaving me. Maybe pulling the sword from the stone would help with my mission… or maybe not. Maybe I just needed to stick with what I was looking for before.

"The kingdom has to have a library." I plotted out my plan. I would sneak into the kingdom and find the library. All of the guards would be busy at the tournament so that was one thing I didn't have to worry about. I would be able to avoid Ector and Kay too.

I walked in the hut and stopped when I saw my mother sitting in an old chair. "Hey mom, can I go spend the rest of my money in the market?"

She sat up in the chair. "Will you go to the market only?"

"Yes." I lied.

She pondered and wouldn't cease to stare into my eyes. She finally broke the silence. "Very well then, you may go." She looked down again.

I ran to the market area without stopping. I saw that all of the merchant stands were abandoned. I imagined everyone was at the tournament. I stopped in the center of the area when I saw and heard eight girls talking about the sword.

"What if the kingdom is tricking us about how the king will be chosen?"

"Perhaps they will choose a king with a knight's physique more than his true strength to pull out a sword."

"The guards will simply find a man that they like and somehow assist him in pulling the sword out."

One of the girls, who looked about fifteen, stopped in her tracts. "Enough! The kingdom will remain fair and just."

The other seven shook their heads. "The kingdom has never shown itself just."

I slowly walked to the girls. They all stared at me, but I stared at the fifteen-year-old. She blushed and used her fan to cover her face.

I stepped closer and looked into her green eyes. "Have we seen each other before?" I admit asking that made the moment awkward, but it was a legit question.

She stepped back and looked at the other girls for help in how to respond.

One of the girls stepped in front of her. "Our sister would rather die than converse with the likes of you."

I stepped forward again. "What is her name?" I asked the girl in front ignoring her comment.

"Are you really that stubborn?" One of the girls asked.

"He does resemble a mule." Another joked.

They all laughed, even the green-eyed girl.

I ignored the girls' insults. "I would rather resemble a mule than any of you girls, well except her with no name."

They stopped laughing. The green-eyed girl stepped in front of her so-called sisters. "I believe you find yourself to be a true man."

"Man?" One of the girls whispered to the others.

"Yes." I said answering the green-eyed girl.

She removed her fan from in front of her face. "Then I challenge you. Pull the sword from the stone and I will honestly answer all of your questions you have for me."

I studied her deep gaze until she blinked. I cleared my throat. "What if… somehow… I can't pull the sword from the stone?"

"Then you will be my family's servant until your death." When she said those words, her sisters snickered.

"I accept your challenge." I said without hesitation. Her and her sisters walked pass me smiling. I could hear their giggles as they passed. I didn't know where the castle was so I planned on running in a straight line. My plan worked, eventually I found the castle.

The stone walkway led to the castle guarded by two knights in front of the drawbridge. The moat around the tower unstirred as two crocodiles appeared. I slowly walked along the walkway as the two knights' laughter pounded in my eardrums. The crocodiles dropped their jaws as I stopped walking.

"You think you can pull the sword from the stone?" One of the knights asked still laughing.

I swallowed my anger. "Yes."

The other knight bent down in laughter. "Truly this is a glorious day."

"Indeed." The other said. "Now be on your way peasant. You cannot do such a thing."

"Neither can you." I fired back. That really wasn't the best thing to say. The two knights grabbed my arms and lifted me up over the moat. "Say that again peasant." One of them said directly in my ear.

I squirmed and they held on tighter. Then their heads turned and they dropped me on the walkway instead of in the moat. I stood up and saw why I was dropped. The eight girls I saw at the market walked over to us.

The knights adjusted themselves as the girls walked to them. "Do you girls plan on testing your true strength?" One asked in a kind joking voice.

They laughed even though his joke wasn't funny. The girls stopped laughing when they saw me.

The knights turned to me. "We told you to leave peasant."

"Brother!" The green-eyed girl said giving me a hug. "Where have you been?"

"Uh…" I didn't catch on at first. "Oh! I… I uh… I journeyed to the market. I thought you would come to this place so…"

"Your brother you say?" One of the knights asked.

The other girls nodded out of synch. The girl stopped hugging me. "Please forgive him." She told the knights. "He is like a mule."

The knights laughed again. "Enter." They stepped aside and the drawbridge fell.

The eight girls and I entered a crowded arena. The area we entered resembled a jousting arena. Red dirt covered the ground and led to brick stands. A box placed up high over the stands was covered in velvet cloth. A golden chair accompanied by a golden crown sat in the center of the box.

The green-eyed girl stopped me. "You are going to thank me, yes?"

"Thank you." I said. "Now, who are you?"

She shook her head. "Pull the sword from the stone and we will converse." Her and her sisters walked away.

I looked through the crowd of knights and saw Kay. He was standing next in line to pull the sword. I myself would've gotten in the line, but the line was too long.

The man at the stone pulled the sword until he was fever-ish and exhausted, but he failed miserably. He ran off crying… poor guy.

 Kay stepped forward and faced the crowd. "Behold! A new king emerges!" He yelled in boastfulness.

The crowd yelled in agreement.

I ran to Kay before he could attempt to pull the sword. "Kay."

He snapped his head at me. "Arthur? How did you…"

"Listen, I need to try this." Why get in line when you can skip? I thought to myself as I begged Kay to let me take his place.

He jabbed his elbow in my stomach. "Go home." He placed his right hand on the sword and shot his left hand up in the air.

The audience yelled and applauded again. Kay inhaled and exhaled deeply. The crowd fell into a hush. Kay pulled at the sword.

Nothing.

He tried his left hand.

Nothing.

He tried both hands.

Nothing.

The audience murmured and Kay started to sweat in embarrassment. He tried pulling the sword with both hands again, and again, and again.

Nothing.

He stopped pulling and the crowd gasped. "No. No! NO! I am supposed to be king!" He yelled to no one particular person.

While he was mourning to the crowd, I got in front of him. I set my right hand on the sword and sighed. My eyes closed and I saw Libra and Cancer sitting in a back to back position as if they were mediating.

My eyes opened and everyone was watching me. Kay grabbed my shoulder. "Do not attempt." He said in a threatening tone.

I shrugged off his hand and looked at the sword. I pulled slightly and the sword moved. I pulled more and more until the sword was no longer in the stone. It resided in my hand as the audience erupted in excruciating cheer.

Kay drew his sword from his sheath and threw the sword on the ground. He walked off as Ector ran pass him. Ector grabbed my shoulders and smiled. "Arthur, you have done it! You are king!" Ector faced the crowd and pointed at me. "Long live King Arthur!"

I gulped and looked at the sword. King Arthur. I thought to myself. The story of the sword in the stone... King Arthur! I looked at the crowd and Ector. "Yeah I got to go!" I ran out of the arena.

I ran pass the two knights as they applauded me. I ran and ran and ran. I was running because I needed help. King Arthur was a story. Or was it real? Regardless it would've happened centuries ago. I needed answers. I needed the green-eyed girl, somebody. I stopped running when I entered a forest. I needed a quiet place to think. The forest would be perfect… so I thought.

Identity Crisis

I sat down by a small puddle of water in the forest. I reached into my bag and opened the book of magic and sighed. I flipped the pages over and over again. I needed to make a portal. I needed a portal back to my time and age where America and all the other countries, continents, islands I knew existed. I also needed the green-eyed girl. She had to be who I was thinking she was. She had to be.

I heard horse's hooves behind me in the distance and I jumped up. I ran and hid behind bushes as a carriage passed by. I saw a man in a velvet robe speaking to a boy around my age. The boy shook his head repeatedly as the man spoke.

When they were a good distance away I slowly and quietly followed them. I don't know why I did, but I did. I just had a feeling that I had to follow them. I had a feeling they could help me. A man that looked like that should have some information.

I was crouched down behind the carriage when it came to a quick halt. I accidently hit the carriage and the book fell out of my hand as I fell to the ground. A man dressed all in black was holding a whip tightly in his right hand. I looked up at his top hat and tried to stand up.

He laid his foot on my chest so I would stay down. He cracked his whip beside me and laughed when he saw the fear in my eyes.

"Fredrick!" The man in a velvet robe said getting out the carriage. "Do not frighten this lad." The man's voice was hearty.

The man lifted his foot from my chest. He then bowed to the other man. "My apologies." He glanced at me and did a side grin. He walked back to the front of the carriage.

I stood up and brushed myself off. "Thank you." I said to the man.

The man raised a thick brown eyebrow. "You are welcome."

"Father make haste!" A boy said stepping out of the carriage. He looked at me and rolled his eyes. "He hit the carriage? He is obviously a peasant. Why would you stop for the likes of him?"

"Pollux, get back in the carriage." The man said getting back inside himself. When he said Pollux, I literally heard bells go off in my head.

The black-haired boy stuck his head out at me from the carriage. "Try to stop me." He said in a very quiet menacing tone. He placed his head back in the carriage and the whip cracked. The two horses pulled the carriage off leaving me in the dust.

I turned and bent down to pick up the book. I placed my hand on the book and heard a girl laugh. I looked up and saw the eight girls.

"You are reading about magic?" One of the girls said.

"Of course, someone like him would."

"What do you girls want?" I asked in annoyance.

The green-eyed girl stepped forward. "I will answer your questions now."

I placed the book in my bag. "It's about time." I said to her with a sigh of relief.

The other seven left us.

The girl sat down elegantly on a tree stump and I sat in front of her with less class of course.

"Where is your sword?" She asked.

"What sword?" I asked. The sword! I left it somewhere!

"Lost?" She asked.

"Yes, I am lost. And you don't have to talk in that accent anymore. No one else is around."

"What are you talking about?" She said continuing to speak in the British accent like her sisters.

"Sofia, you can stop the act."

"Sofia?" She asked confused.

"Samantha, maybe." I corrected myself.

"Okay I am not she of your name."

"Who's your dad?" I asked her.

"Why would you need to know that?"

"You said you would answer my questions if I pulled the sword out the stone. So, answer who is your dad."

She looked down. "My father's name was Absalom."

"What's your mom's name?"

"I do not know." She said looking at the sky.

"How can you not know your mother name?"

"I am the youngest of my sisters. My mother died giving birth to me. My sisters never told me her name."

"And you never asked?"

"No. I thought it better for me to not know." She made straight eye contact with me.

"Who was that man in the carriage?"

"What man?"

"He wore a velvet robe and had a boy in the carriage with him. The boy's name was Pollux." When I said his name, I heard the bells again.

"I did not see them. I apologize."

"Okay then, what's your name?"

"Maria."

"Okay Maria, who am I?"

She raised an eyebrow and shrugged her shoulders. "I don't really know, I just met you today. But I did hear people call you Arthur when you pulled the sword out the stone."

"I'm not Arthur. My father isn't Ector. My brother isn't Kay. I'm Lancaster. My father is Aquarius. I thought I had a brother, but I don't."

"Aquarius?"

"Yes, my father is Aquarius."

She reached at my side and took the book out of my bag. She carefully flipped the pages. When she stopped flipping the pages, she turned the book facing me. I looked and saw a picture of my father. The page had a spell to control metal.

"You think you're his son?" She asked pointing in the book.

"I am his son. He's my father. I had his Gem but he took it from me."

"Gem, she said confusingly?"

The earth being destroyed should've happened by now. "Never mind. Look… Maria, you said your father is Absalom?"

"My father was Absalom." She said softly.

"Absalom? Why does that name sound familiar?"

"He was a carpenter." She told me.

"What are your other sister's names?"

"Their names are Constance, Phoebe, Onyx, Hope, Agnes, Sapphire, and Trinity." She said counting on her fingers.

"That is the order from eldest to youngest."

"And you're the youngest?"

"Yes I am."

"And you don't have any brothers?"

"No, I don't."

The seven sisters then filed up behind Maria. She stood and brushed the dirt off of her dress.

One of the sisters eyed me up and down repeatedly. "We found your sword back over there king."

"Why didn't you just get it and bring it to me?"

"We tried but failed."

I nodded then looked at Maria. "Thank you." I walked toward the direction of the sword.

"Wait!" Maria said.

I turned around.

"Do you have a place to sleep tonight?" Maria asked.

I thought about my answer. If I were to go home Kay would give me a hard time. Ector and his wife would praise me, so Kay would be even more jealous. But there was no guarantee these girls could be trusted. "No, I don't."

Maria grabbed my arm. "You can come home with us then."

"Maria!" One of the sisters said rudely.

"We don't want him in our home!"

"He reads about magic and he may use it on us!"

"I trust him." Maria said. "He means us no harm. He is like a ship without a sail."

The other girls whispered amongst themselves then they all agreed to let me stay with them for the night. I went back and picked up the sword then I was arm-lead to an area of brick houses… I mean brick mansions. The mansions were square and two-story, and had wooden doors. The girls escorted me into one of the many brick houses. They began to show me around.

When you walk through the front door, the dining area was to the left and the kitchen was to the right. Straight ahead to the left passed the stairs was a ballroom. Straight ahead to the right passed the stairs was another entrance to the ballroom.

Up the white marble stairs you would have found an in-finite number of doors. Behind each door to the left were bedrooms. To the right were bathrooms, a study, an observatory, and a library. They wouldn't take me any farther than the library.

The eight girls led me to the left and after passing eight-bedroom doors they stopped in front of a door. One of the girls opened the door and I stepped in. "Good night." They said in unison and then the door slammed.

I walked to the window and rested my forehead on the glass. I threw the sword and my messenger bag on the ground and I closed my eyes. Am I supposed to get rid of the sword? Are these eight girls the ones I'm supposed to stop? Do I even need the magic book?

I would ask myself more questions the next morning. Right then I needed to sleep. I felt that it was safe to say that my first day in Grassland was… eventful. I had no doubt that the remainder of my time there would be nothing short of it. When I woke up the next morning, I found myself sleeping under soft cotton blankets. I woke up in an actual bed opposed to the ground. The light from the window spread to the door. The birds greeted me with a song. I kicked the blankets off of myself and stood. I stretched and picked up my bag. I set it on the chair in front of the bed and picked up the sword.

I mused at the golden gem-incrusted handle. The bronze blade blinded me as I held it to the sunlight. The sword felt weightless. It was much lighter than a feather. I touched the tip of the blade and the bedroom door opened slowly.

Maria entered smiling and carrying clothes. "I thought you would be awake by now. Good morning."

I set the sword beside my bag. "Good morning."

She walked to me and handed me the clothes. "These are… were my fathers. I think you might be able to fit them."

"Thank you." I said genuinely.

She nodded and walked to the door. "Constance is making breakfast come down when you are done."

"I will."

She shut the door softly and I sighed. I looked at the black pants, green shirt, and gray robe. "How could a carpenter afford all of this?"

I went to the bathroom and took the longest shower of my life. When I was done, I put the clothes on and went back to my room. I set my old clothes in a corner and grabbed the sword and my bag. I made my way to the dining room. A table sat in the middle of the room. Four chairs lined each side and a chair at each end. Six of the girls were already seated while the other two girls placed the food. A turkey sat in the center of a circle that consisted of numerous plates of fruits and vegetables.

Not an ordinary breakfast. I thought to myself. I was used to toast and eggs for breakfast, not a full turkey. When the other two girls were seated, they all stared at me. I walked to one of the chairs at the end of the table. I pulled it back and was about to sit down when I heard…

"Stop!"

"That is father's chair!"

"Do not touch it!"

"I'm sorry!" I yelled back. I didn't yell in anger; it was in a tone of shock. I gently pushed the chair back in.

Maria shook her head. "He can sit there if he wants to."

"Maria!"

"Have you no compassion for our father?!"

"It is a chair." She said slowly and calmly. She looked at me. "Sit."

I gulped. "I can sit in the chair at the other end. I don't have to sit here."

"Sit." She said again.

I sighed and sat down.

The other seven shook their heads at me. Maria smiled. "If father was still with us, he would have giving his chair to Lancaster."

"Father is not here." One of the sisters responded.

"He would long for us to be kind if he were here." Maria reminded her.

"Wait a minute." I said. "Did you just call me Lancaster?"

"Yes. You said it is your name." Maria said still smiling.

"Can we eat now?" One of the girls asked.

"Guest first." Maria said. It was as if her smile was permanent.

The other girls scoffed and rolled their eyes.

"I insist that you girls go first." I insisted.

"You are quite the gentleman." Marie joked.

After we all ate Maria insisted on taking me to their library. The others girls insisted on tagging along with us. While we were in the library, I learned each girl's name, age, and their personality.

Constance was nineteen and only wanted to help and protect her sisters. Phoebe was eighteen and always wanted to learn. Other people thought her and Onyx were twins. They were both the same age and had the same personality, but they weren't twins. Hope was seventeen and her name fit her. Sixteen-year-old Agnes always wanted to either get into trouble or be the trouble. She was rude and definitely a tomboy. Sapphire was also sixteen, but she wasn't like Agnes. Sapphire was the opposite of Agnes. Trinity was fifteen and timid. She never said much. She was very shy and would occasionally burst into tears for reasons no one knew. Then there was Maria. I didn't get to know much about her except that she was thirteen. That is all she would tell me.

I looked around at the books. I was only on the third row of books. The library had winding stairs that Agnes would climb then jump down from while Constance yelled at her. Onyx and Phoebe sat beside each other and started to read the five books they had stacked beside them. Hope patted Trinity's back as she silently cried. Sapphire elegantly walked around the library. Maria stood beside me as I scanned through the books.

"What are you looking for?" She asked.

"Anything that'll help me out." I said without looking at her.

"Help you with what?"

"Anything that will help my figure out why I am in Grassland." I responded.

"Lancaster, you claim to be the son of Aquarius."

"Yeah."

"Do you yourself believe that?"

"Yes. I was told that."

She put her hand on my shoulder and I stopped looking at the books. I looked into her dark green eyes. "You shouldn't believe everything you're told." She said softly and without an accent.

"What happened to your accent?"

Sapphire then spotted me. "Please excuse my interruption, but will you aid me Mr. Lancaster?"

"Um… sure." I said. "But you can just call me Lancaster."

Sapphire gently pulled me to the library window up the stairs. "Who are you?" She asked looking out the floor to ceiling window.

"I'm Lancaster. I'm the son of Aquarius." I said.

Her eyes widened. "Aquarius? The Zodian god of metal?"

"Yeah, the one and only."

She did a faint grin. "Have you gone mad?"

"It's true." I said.

"The Zodians do not have children."

"Wait a minute. How do you know about the Zodians?"

"We all do." Onyx said. She motioned for me to come to her.

I walked to her and Phoebe and the others did the same. Onyx handed me a book and I sat in the chair beside her.

"Though some may think they are a lie, Zodians live." Phoebe told me.

"I know." I replied. "I'm Aquarius's son. How many times do I have to say it?"

"They are all childless." Onyx said.

"No. They have children." After I said that statement I started thinking. When we were on Mercy's plane Sofia told me that she couldn't tell who she was the daughter of. No one is supposed to know about the Zodians children. If only I would've known about that sooner. It was too late for me to deny that I was Aquarius' son at this point.

"You are a donkey." Agnes said to me. As she sat in the chair in front of me.

Constance slapped the back of Agnes's head.

"Ow!" Agnes yelled.

"Continue." Constance said kindly to me.

"I feel that I need to be honest with you eight." So then, I told them. I told them everything from the day we planned on leaving to find the Temple of Zodia to when I met them.

They all had a blank expression on their faces. The room and their expressions seemed to have paused. Finally, I couldn't take the silence. "Do you believe me or not?"

Maria blinked. "You really think I am... Sofia?"

"Yeah. You two have the same eyes and hair."

"I believe you Lancaster." Onyx said.

"We all will help you in anyway." Phoebe added.

"Thank you." I picked up the sword. "Is there a place where I can practice with this?"

Hope, still comforting Trinity, pointed out the window. "Back there."

While the seven girls watched me train (Agnes was busy playing with insects) my mind kept on going back to Maria and what she said. "You shouldn't believe everything you're told." Maybe she is Sofia and she's just lying. But why would she lie? And why would she say such a thing?

My concentration was broken when Sapphire gracefully placed her hand on my shoulder. My head turned slightly.

She smiled. "You train like my father used to."

"He was a carpenter and a swordsman?" I asked.

"No. The world saw Absalom as a carpenter, but his daughters and wife saw him for who he truly was."

"A swordsman?"

She leaned in and whispered in my ear, "The sword you hold is his. He wasn't a mere swordsman." She leaned back. "Follow." She started walking into the house.

I followed her until Maria stopped us. "Where are you taking him?" She asked Sapphire.

Sapphire did a faint grin. "Do not concern yourself with that, Maria." She turned her head. "Go comfort Trinity."

Maria rolled her eyes. "Fine." She walked to Trinity.

Sapphire brought me back into the library and told me to sit down. While I was sitting, I watched her fumble through the books. She would take one off the shelf then put it back without looking at the cover. After watching her for a while I finally asked her if she needed help.

"Do you need any help?" I yelled to her while she was up the stairs.

She looked down from the balcony. "Yes. I could use your assistance."

When I made my way up the stairs, she had three books sitting on the table. Each book had a V on the cover.

"There are seven more books like these. Can you help me find them?"

"Of course."

We looked for the other seven books. It felt like hours had passed when we found them. We set all the books on the table down the stairs.

Sapphire closed her eyes. "You are the son of Aquarius?"

"Yes."

"Then you know of the one called Virgo?"

"Yeah. At first, she didn't like me, but now she kind of does... at least I think she does."

Her eyes widened. "You did not tell us that you met her."

"Yeah, well I've met all of the Zodians."

"Even... Cancer?" She stammered.

"Yeah. Why wouldn't I meet him?"

"The fool has been banished."

"Well in my time he's back with the other Zodians." So, I was in the pass. But in the pass, there were more than three countries. Right?

She nodded and looked down at the books. "These books were written by Virgo herself."

"Virgo wrote a book? That's a huge shocker."

"It's said that some consist of her and the Zodians origin."

"Have you read them yet?"

"No."

"Why not?"

She sat down in a chair in front of the table. "The letters, they are unreadable."

I sat beside her and opened one of the books. "What language is this?"

"I do not know. Neither does Phoebe or Onyx. Those two are usually geniuses at things like this."

Leave it to Virgo to write a book that no one can read. I pulled the magic book out of my bag. "Maybe she wrote this one too."

"Does it show the Zodians and how to conjure their powers?" She asked.

"Yeah."

"Intriguing."

"Wait a minute. Why are you giving me the extra help? Not that I'm complaining, but why?"

"You need it, so I will supply it."

"But why exactly?"

She closed the book. "My other sisters do not know of what I am about to inform you of. Do not tell them, ever."

"I won't. You have my word, Sapphire."

"Father himself constructed that sword. He thought only mother knew of it, but I overheard them talking. Father presented himself as a carpenter, but he was a swordsman. When he was laid to rest, I found the sword hidden in his study. I tried to pick it up, but I failed. The next day when I returned, it was gone. Recently I heard of a sword in a stone. I knew what it truly was. Therefore, I knew that only a true man, like my father, could lift it. I convinced my sisters to come and watch with me. We went… and you pulled the sword from the stone."

I gulped. "Okay, let me get this straight. Your dad somehow made a sword that only he could lift. When he died you found it then it was all of a sudden gone. Then it appears again years later in a stone and I'm the guy that's supposed to have it."

"Yes."

"Wait a minute. Is Arthur or Lancaster supposed to have the sword?"

She ran her hand through my hair. "Whoever you truly are." She whispered in my ear.

Just then we heard footsteps. "Hide the books!" Sapphire whispered.

We both quickly hid the books. I put my magic book back in my bag right when Maria showed herself to us.

Sapphire just finished hiding the last book when she asked, "Maria, what are you doing?"

Maria walked around silently. She passed by me three times without looking me in my eyes. On the fourth time she stopped. She was looking me in the eyes now. "Who are you?"

I searched her dark-green eyes to see if I could figure out what she meant. I already told her and the others who I was. Why would she ask again? "I'm Lancaster son of Aquarius."

"For how long?"

"In my time, thirteen years. In your time, I'm not sure."

"Who are you?"

"I just told you. I'm…"

"Maria!" Sapphire said cutting me off. "Go see if any of our sisters require assistance."

"They do not." Maria said still staring at me.

"That was not a suggestion, it was a command."

Maria nodded. "As you wish." She left the library.

"Do you think she heard us talking?" I asked Sapphire as I sat back down.

"Perhaps. Still, the others must not know. I will take care of Maria, in the meantime start trying to read Virgo's books."

Then she left. I gathered the books together and placed as many as possible in my bag. I hand carried the others. I looked down both ends of the hallway before I left. It was clear, so I ran. I ran to my bedroom door and opened it without dropping the books in my hand. When I shut the door, I realized that… it wasn't my room.

Trinity sat at the edge of her bed and cried. I was at first going to ask her if she was okay, but I decided not to. I probably should have asked, but I didn't. I left as quickly as I entered.

I opened another door and saw that it was my room. I closed the door and saw that there was no lock so I couldn't lock the door. I set the books and my bag on the bed and took off my cape.

I picked up the first volume and turned to the first page. The writing was written in a very weird language.

"What are you saying Virgo?!" I lied back on the bed. "What are you saying?" I tried thinking like Virgo, but I couldn't do it. I just couldn't. I laid the book on my stomach and put my hands behind my head.

Virgo isn't stupid. Why did she write these books on the Zodians origin? And why didn't any of the Zodians tell me about the books? And why would she write the books in a weird language? And why can I lift the sword? And how come Sapphire knows about the books but her sisters don't? I drifted off to sleep.

My eyes opened and the evening sun blinded my eyes. I squinted and sat up. I had no idea what to do. I was done living in whatever century I was in. I was done playing this guessing game of questions. I didn't want to save the world. I just wanted to go home and enjoy my last days on earth. So, I did something unusual for me. I stood up and knelt down at the bed. I folded my hands together and closed my eyes, to pray.

"Great Libra the Zodian god of Balance, I pray to you for one reason… I am done. I am done being in this century. I am no hero. I am no god. I am only a boy that wants to return home. Yes, I have failed you. Yes, I have failed my father. Yes, I have failed the other Elders and my friends. Please, take me home. Take me away from this place. Let me live my not normal but okay life. The world needs a real hero… not me. Only gods can do miracles… not the sons of gods." I opened my eyes and looked up. "Did you hear that? Great Libra did you hear my prayer?"

I stood up and exhaled. I sat at the edge of the bed and waited. I waited for something to happen. "Maybe I should've stayed in the After Life."

I tapped my foot repeatedly until I saw that the sun was going down. Maybe prayers don't get answered. I stood up and opened the door. I walked down the stairs and entered the ball-room. It was much bigger than I thought it would be. The ceiling was lined with portraits of baby angels, the walls were covered in abstract art, and the grand piano sat in the right corner. The window covered the entire back wall.

I walked to the piano and sat on the bench. Any time now Libra. I looked around the room again. I had a feeling that my prayer wouldn't be answered. After sitting at the bench for the longest time, an idea popped into my head. It was crazy and stupid, but all my ideas were. I ran into my room and shut the door. I picked up the sword and sighed. I held the tip to my stomach. "Aries, get me the heck out of here." The only way I could escape that place was death. So, I stabbed myself.

The Eight Ladies

"What!" I yelled. I didn't even feel a thing. On top of that, the sword didn't even pierce my skin. "Fine. Let's try it this way." I tried cutting my throat but it was as if the swords blade was made out of silk.

I cut at the wall and left a mark. So, the sword could cut things, but not me. I collapsed on the floor and looked at the gold gems on the handle of the sword. As I gazed into it my mind went blank. I saw nothing but the strange symbols from the books. They floated around in my mind then disappeared. Floated around then disappeared. I would've watched the symbols longer, but I was interrupted.

"Lancaster!" Maria was shaking my shoulder.

I sat up. "What? What?"

"Come quickly!" She darted out the door.

I stood up and ran after her. When we made it to the front door, the man I saw before in the carriage was standing in the doorway. He laughed as Constance repeatedly told him to leave.

"What's going on?" I asked.

Constance whipped her head around. "This abomination is attempting to cause us to leave our home."

"What?" I asked.

The man laughed some more. "As your newest king I am granted power. Because I have power, I am permitted to take what I desire. Therefore, I see that your house is magnificent. So, it is mine."

"You can't take their home." I said walking closer to him.

He raised his eyebrow. "Aren't you the boy who hit my carriage?"

"He's not only that boy," Maria started, "he is the king."

The man laughed once more. "How is he king?"

I held up the sword.

He had a confused look on his face.

"There was a tournament." I said as if he should have already known. "Whoever would be able to pull this sword from the stone would be the newest king."

"And you are the king?"

"Yes."

"Where's your crown?"

"Where's your crown?" I asked hoping that would throw him off.

He clapped his hands twice and the man with the whip walked up holding a gold crown.

The man grinned at me. "Now where did you say your crown is?"

Darn he's good! "Look, you're not taking their house away from them. If you want to be king, fine. But you leave these girls alone."

"And if I refuse?" The "king" said.

I took the sword and cut his arm in a flash. He backed up in pain leaving a trail of blood. The man dressed in black dropped the crown and removed his whip from under his arm.

He cracked the whip at my sword. I backed up then ran at him. He cracked the whip again and the sword blocked it. I then dropped the sword and ran at him again. Then I used something I learned from football try-outs. I tackled him the football way.

When he fell, I picked up my sword and put it to his throat. "Yield." If Coach Hammond could see me now, I would definitely be on the football team.

The "king" stood. "Stop. Let us leave."

"Sir Lancaster." The man under my sword whispered to me. "Let me go for Madame Virgo's sake."

I looked down at him. I only knew one man that would ever call me sir. "Fredrick?"

The man nodded. "Okay?"

I took my sword away from his neck and looked at the "king". "What's your name?"

"Eddington. Louie Eddington." The man said fearfully and un-kingly.

I looked at the girls who stood motionless. "Take king Eddington, I mean Mr. Eddington and bandage him up." I said Mr. on purpose.

"No, we will not! He just tried to take away our home!" Constance reminded me.

"Do as I say. Help him."

All the girls reluctantly helped Mr. Eddington inside and started bandaging him up.

I looked at Fredrick. "Were you brought here by Libra too?"

"No. Madame Virgo recently informed me that the son of Aquarius would soon come here."

"How'd you know it was me?"

He smiled. "Madame Virgo said that Lancaster would be the one wielding the sword from the stone."

"So, she's in on it with Libra?"

"In on what Sir Lancaster?"

"Never mind. Look, where's that boy?"

"What boy, oh, Sir Pollux?"

"Yeah."

"Sir Pollux." Fredrick called to the carriage.

The black-haired boy exited from the carriage. "What Fredrick?" He asked walking up to us. He immediately stopped walking when he saw me.

"You again."

"Yeah, me again. Who are you?" I asked him.

"Why do you care who I am?"

"Because, your father has an accent and talks like everyone else that lives here, but you don't. Why is that?"

"Sir Lancaster, perhaps we should go inside and ensure that King Eddington is being treated correctly." Fredrick said to me.

I stared into Pollux's gray eyes for a few seconds. He stared at me the same. He wanted to know about me more than I wanted to know about him. I could tell.

"Let's go Fredrick." I said putting my hand on his shoulder. We both walked into the house. I stopped and turned to Pollux. "Don't you want to see if your father is okay?"

"Louie will be fine." He said walking to the carriage. "If he's not, tell me and I'll find a nice shady tree to bury him under."

I shook my head. "The son of a "king" and yet he has no compassion for people... then again, neither does his father."

Mr. Eddington was okay. The girls sat him down in one of the bedrooms and wrapped his wounds. All the girls laid him down in the bed. When I walked in Mr. Eddington looked up at me.

"Can you girls give me and Mr. Eddington a moment?" I asked them.

They nodded and left.

Mr. Eddington sat up. "You wound me, then aid me. Why?"

"I'm not a killer... I'm just a guy who needs help."

"You have aided me, so I will aid you."

"Are you really a king?" I asked in a curious tone.

He went silent. "I have lost my throne but became king again here.

"How?" I was thinking, if there was a king why have the tournament to find a king.

"How can I aid you?" He asked refusing to answer me about how he could be king.

"I don't think you can help me… unless you can read symbols." I wasn't going to pressure him on answering my question, at least not now.

I collected all of the books and took Mr. Eddington to the library. I showed him one of books. After looking at the page for ten minutes he finally blinked.

"I haven't seen these markings since I was a lad." He sat back in his chair.

"Do you remember how to read them?" I asked trying not to sound desperate.

"I recognize some, but not all. Perhaps I may be able to translate this page, but I will need time."

"Take all the time you need… and… thanks." I said genuinely.

He nodded and looked down at the page again.

I must've falling asleep when he was studying the page in the book. When I opened my eyes, my face was in a puddle of drool and it was morning. Mr. Eddington caught my gaze. He looked wide-awake and he was smiling. I sat up and wiped the side of my face clear of saliva.

He looked at me and his smile widened. He slapped my back. "I have been successful at decrypting one of the books!"

I rubbed my back. "Really? That's great."

He handed me the book. "It took all night but it was worth it."

"So, you read the book?"

"Yes, but it speaks of the Elders of Zodia."

"What about the other books? What do those talk about?"

"I do not know. I was only able to decipher the first book."

"Can you show me how to decipher the symbols?"

"But of course."

It took from dawn to noon, but finally I understood the symbols. After he was done teaching me, King Eddington left (he has now earned my respect to be called "king"). However, he didn't leave without apologizing to us for causing us the trouble. We all forgave him... all of us except for Constance.

When he left, I returned to my room and sat beside the bed. I had a lot of reading to do and all the time in the world to do it. The first sentence of the book would be translated to: "This is the unabridged history of the Elders of Zodia." After reading the first three pages I realized that I already read that book.

Back when I was in Germany, dad had books about the Zodians. I was able to read them by stealing them from Peter's bedroom when he wasn't looking. I got to read them without having to be secretive when I was eleven. So, the first three books in that series I already read. The fourth book was torn and pages were falling so I had to be as careful as possible:

Being the Zodian goddess of life causes me to involuntarily love nature. Therefore, Capricorn and I are quite good friends, although it is not known. Though he did not assist me in recreating the earth, I still respect him... I still highly respect him. After helping recreate the earth, I came to earth as a mortal. That was the first biggest mistake of my life. The second biggest mistake of my life was conceiving a daughter. I named her

Mercy because I prayed that my eternal soul would have mercy upon me. Sadly, my prayer was not answered.

Page 1

To be honest, I tried to have her killed. Taurus had a wife and a daughter. Instead of killing the five-month-old baby he had, I killed the mother. That was the only way for Taurus to come after Mercy. I believed that if I took his wife he would come after my daughter, but if I took his daughter he would come after me. It was not until my second daughter was born when Taurus found out that I killed his wife. He believed that some regular mortal took her life away. Therefore Melissa, my beloved baby daughter, was murdered by him. Since then, Taurus and I have never gotten along. Neither of us has told the other Elders why we have complications.

Page 2

When Melissa was killed, I almost regretted killing Taurus's wife… almost. I did not want a third regret. I wanted my beloved daughter back. Mercy was and still is and may forever hate me. I am okay with that however. Aries will not bring Melissa back to me unless I tell him how she died. I believe he knows how and why she died and he is just pretending that he does not know. I will get Melissa back one day. Taurus will get over his wife's murder eventually. She will probably be fine. After all I did speak with her once. She was kind, generous, and perky. All the things I hated and will probably always hate. No wonder I killed her and not her daughter. Sofia, her beautiful daughter who will be a spoiled brat when she gets older, will be fine without a mother. Maria was never like a real mother anyway. She would always leave Taurus and…

Maria! Maria is Sofia's future mother! Or pass mother! No wonder she looks like Sofia! But was I in the pass or present? If I was in the pass that meant Mercy hadn't been born yet.

Meaning I could probably stop the whole situation. But if I was in the future then…

I ran to the kitchen and found Maria, Constance, Phoebe, and Onyx preparing that night's meal. They didn't stop what they were doing when I entered. They didn't even look at me.

"Maria, I need to talk to you." I said.

"Not now Lancaster." She said as she grabbed a knife and started chopping the vegetables. "Later."

"I need to talk to you now. Your future is in danger! Possibly."

"Later."

I grabbed her arm and she dropped the knife. "No, now." I pulled her out the kitchen and sat her down on the steps.

"What? What about my future?" She asked without interest.

I inhaled. "In a few years you're going to marry the Zodian god of strength named Taurus. You two are going to have a daughter and you're going to name her Samantha Sofia and the Zodian goddess of life, named Virgo, is going to kill you because she's going to hate her first daughter named Mercy. So now I have to either stop Virgo from coming to earth and meeting Edward von Tomb or keep you safe until she finally decides to leave you alone." I exhaled.

She stared at me without expression.

"Possibly… I think I'm in the pass. Or maybe the future… do you believe me or not!"

She looked down. "When will I wed Taurus?"

I sat beside her. "I'm not sure." I thought about it. "It doesn't make sense though."

"What does not make sense?"

"Like I just said, I don't know if I'm in the pass or present. Look, all I know is that it's either you're going to be over a thousand years old when you have Sofia, or she was over a thousand years old when I first met her. I don't know, I'm still confused myself."

She put her hand on my shoulder and laughed. "Neither of those seems logical."

"I know, but it has to happen somehow."

"Agnes stop, this insolence!" Sapphire exclaimed and she came running down the stairs.

Agnes, not to far back from her, chased after her as she held a rat in her hands. "Just speak to my newest pet Sapphire." She said jokingly as she ran in between Maria and me.

Sapphire quickly turned around and with great speed grabbed me and used me as a shield. "Agnes, stop!" Sapphire warned.

I sighed. "Agnes, put the rat outside."

Agnes rolled her eyes. "I can't allow Raphael to go into this cursed world."

"Raphael?" Sapphire said peeking over my shoulder. "Agnes, you should be smart enough to know better than that…"

"You are a true fool." Constance said as she exited the kitchen.

Agnes eyed Constance. "Raphael, fathers' brother, was a rat so this is quite fitting."

By the look in Constance eyes I could tell she was holding in her anger. "What if father was standing before you at this moment? What do you think he would say?"

Agnes looked down.

Constance sighed. "For father to hear one of his cherished daughters curse his only brother would cause him great pain."

Agnes lifted her eyes. "Everyone has their own opinion."

"Not everyone should share their own opinion."

"Not everyone should watch two sisters argue and say nothing to stop it." I said hoping to stop them. "So, how about dinner?" I asked trying to change the subject.

"I agree." Sapphire said playing along. "Perhaps Onyx and Phoebe require an aid in the kitchen."

Agnes handed me the rat and walked up the stairs. Constance, obviously pleased with herself for winning the argument, returned to the kitchen. Sapphire hid behind Maria as she watched the rat squirm in my hands. "Please, please get that abomination away from this place."

I set the rat on my shoulder. "None of you told me that your dad had a brother."

"You did not ask." Maria responded.

"Tell me about him." I said sitting back down on the steps.

Maria sat beside me. "There is nothing to speak of. Raphael was nothing more than an unruly uncle."

"He prided himself on his looks." Sapphire added as she stared at the rat. "He had to look his best." She sat beside Maria.

"Why was he just called a rat?"

Maria and Sapphire smiled at that question. "He personally believed that women should be elegant and considerate. Two main things Agnes lacks. So, he was not…" she paused to find the right word, "pleased with her." Sapphire said.

"Where is he now?" I been waiting anxiously to ask.

"We are not sure." Sapphire said as she finally lifted her gaze away from the rat. "Agnes would say one place but we don't know."

"Just stop it, he is dead" A still little voice said silently and very softly.

Looking at Maria "I see, okay. I'm guessing Constance liked him a lot."

"Yes. He loved her the most." Sapphire said through clenched teeth. "Even though I was always the one who always agreed with him on all things."

"Sapphire, you must allow the pass to stay in the pass." Maria said.

"What was his job, what did he do?"

"He was a…"

"Don't say carpenter." I told them.

Sapphire sighed. "He was a…" She stopped.

"He was a what? A what?" I asked.

"If we told you, you would not believe us." Maria stated with confidence.

"Try me."

"A… magician." Maria said.

"He used… magic?" I asked as the rat squeaked in my ear.

Sapphire nodded. "Though no one knew. He assisted our father into constructing the sword."

"Um… Your sisters weren't supposed to know about the sword." I whispered to her.

Sapphire sighed. "Maria overheard our, what should have been, private conversation."

"Lucky me." Maria said. "Uncle Raphael helped our father by magically binding him and the sword together. That made it impossible for any other being to wield it." They booth stared at me blankly.

"What?"

They both stood. "Only our father would be able to hold that sword."

"And…?"

With smiles they simultaneously said, "You are our father."

"That's impossible!" I said jumping up. "I'm only thirteen! I can't be a father! Technically speaking…"

"Only our father could wield the sword, Lancaster." Maria said smiling.

"So, our father is alive!" Sapphire exclaimed.

"No! Because I am not your father! I went back in time!"

"Or perhaps forward." Onyx said exiting the kitchen. Phoebe walked behind her. "Your voices carry."

"I couldn't have traveled forward. Libra sent me to stop the earth's destruction again."

"Perhaps the threat you spoke to us is here… in perhaps the future. It's hard to say considering we don't know what time you're from." Phoebe said.

The other sisters lined up along the balcony of the stairs. They obviously heard the conversation. They all stared at me without expression.

I shook my head. "Maria is supposed to meet Taurus and they're supposed to have a daughter. That hasn't happened yet… possibly."

"There are others with my name." Maria said.

"But… but…" I was at a loss for words. I couldn't have been their father. I just couldn't be. It wasn't logical with all the facts. Or was it? "What year is it?"

They all looked away from me.

"What year is it?!" I yelled. The rat scurried off my shoulder.

"2065." Trinity said softly. Her sisters stared at her in amazement."

"A.d. or b.c.?" I asked her in particular. I wanted to hear her velveteen voice again.

"I do not understand." Her feminine voice said with complete honesty.

I looked at the others. "A.d. or b.c.?"

They all shrugged.

"Well it has to be…" It couldn't be b.c. If that was the case then everyone would be in robes and writing for a special Book. Maybe Libra did send me forward in time. Maybe I was still thirteen because that was the age I was when Libra sent me, or maybe this whole situation was nothing more than a dream. Maybe I was asleep in my room back in Germany. Maybe I just needed to wake up. Maybe my name really wasn't Lancaster. Maybe I was still Cyrus O'Hara. Maybe my brother really was Peter O'Hara. Maybe Judas was my school bully and Sofia was my only friend.

I guess by the look on my face the girls realized that I was deep in thought. They stared at me quietly and listened intently when I finally spoke to them. I sighed. "Maybe Libra did send me to the future. But my name isn't Absalom. It's Lancaster. Or maybe… maybe Lancaster is a lie too. But the future should have flying cars not three countries that have terrible names."

I looked at each of the girls. "What was your mother's name?"

"Landra." They all said at once.

I fell on the ground and my eyes widened. "If, if I am your father, then… then Landra isn't my mother… she's… my wife. I…I don't understand."

They all crowded around me to make sure I was okay. Looking deeply concerned, Maria said "Are you okay?"

"No, I'm not okay." I told them. "Aquarius lied. So did my friends. Everyone lied about everything. Except maybe my age. I'm young."

"He sent you at thirteen, so you are thirteen." Constance said.

I covered my eyes. "But by now I would be somewhere in my sixties." I then thought of something. "What color were Absalom's eyes?"

"Crimson." Hope said.

"Maybe he had the Aries Gem." I said. "Meaning he could live forever… unless he removed the Gem. But why would he give up immortality?"

"Perhaps for Raphael." Agnes said.

"Where's Raphael buried?" I asked.

"Why do you want to see his grave?" Sapphire asked.

"Just take me to it… fast."

We had to walk three miles but we made it. The girls took me to a cemetery. Sadly, it was nighttime so we were scared… by we I mean me. Though I was scared I tried to think happy thoughts. That didn't work out… at all.

I was thinking the bad thoughts. Like how everyone lied to me. Maybe, maybe I really was Absalom… maybe. There still wasn't enough proof or logic for me. As a just in case I brought the sword. That was a bad idea because that caused me… just for a second… to believe I was Absalom… just for a second. Within that second, they found Raphael's grave.

Dead flowers lay on the grave. The broken tombstone read: Rest in Peace Our Beloved Raphael 2014-2059.

I squatted in front of the grave. "He was only 45? How did he die?"

"Father never said." Sapphire told me. "He told us that he died, but he never said how."

I gathered my thoughts together. Absalom possibly had the Aries Gem meaning he was immortal, but he died. Raphael probably tricked Absalom into removing the Aries Gem then Raphael took the Gem. Maybe at the last moments of his life

Raphael hid the Gem and Absalom killed him. "Were Absalom's eyes always crimson?"

"Yes." Constance said.

"Then… he can't be dead… but I can't be Absalom. I don't have the Aries Gem. My eyes aren't red. Plus, I don't have a real brother." Maybe the Gems took on different forms depending on the person. Maybe… no! No! NO! NO! I am not Absalom! "When did Absalom die?"

"A year after Raphael died." Maria said.

Maybe Absalom was cursed. Maybe his eyes were naturally red. I knelt on top of Raphael's grave. "Where's Absalom's grave?"

They took me to his grave. The inscription on the tombstone was the same as Raphael's only it said Absalom and the years were different.

I knelt down on Absalom's grave. "I am about to prove to all of you that I am not Absalom." I started digging. I would dig up the casket and open it. If a dead guy was inside of it then I wasn't Absalom. If there wasn't a dead guy in it then… I would find another way to show them that I wasn't Absalom.

"Don't dig up our father!" They all protested at once (even Trinity).

"I have to… I have to make sure." I kept digging and digging and digging. I ignored their pleas, yelling, and cursing. I had to prove to them that I wasn't Absalom… and I had to prove that fact to myself.

After what felt like hours of digging, I found the wooden casket. I looked up at the girls. "This is the moment of truth." With their help we got the casket out of the hole.

I rubbed my hands together. I knelt beside the casket and slowly opened it up. There was either one of two things in it.

There was either a man who loved his family and created a magical sword with his brother… or nothing.

I closed my eyes when I opened the casket. I looked at the girls. They stood motionless and pale. I looked down in the casket.

Nothing, it was empty.

Deceitfulness and Lies

"No! There is no way!" I said to no one in particular. There was no way I could be their father! There was no way Landra was my wife! There was no way! "This doesn't make sense!" I looked around. "Where's your mother's grave?!"

"That's enough." Candace said to me.

"No. This isn't enough!" I sighed. "Look, all of you know why I came here. I came here to stop whoever is responsible for the next destruction of the earth." I stood. "I'm just passing through basically." I looked at the casket. "So, really this doesn't matter."

"Not even us?" Trinity asked in a shaky voice.

"What? No… that's not what I… look I just need to find the person. When I do, I'm done here."

"How are you sure?" Hope asked.

"Libra told me…"

"Didn't Libra and the Sacred Twelve also tell you that you are the son of Aquarius? Didn't Libra and the Sacred Twelve also tell you that your mother is Landra?" Maria said.

"Yes but… but…" I sighed. "I have to do what I have to do. I'm here to help stop the earth's destruction… I'm not here to make friends." I touched the sword at my side. "And I am not here to be called a father." I drew the sword and showed it to them. "This means nothing. This is nothing more than a distraction."

"Are we a distraction too?" Trinity said looking down.

I didn't say another word. I walked to the hole where the casket was buried. I dropped the sword in the hole. The tip landed smoothly in the dirt, but not without making a loud cling. I turned to the girls. None of them looked at me. They turned their backs and started walking.

The sword couldn't possibly help me. It was a distraction. I'd forgotten why I was really here. I needed answers, meaning I needed the books. One of them contained information I needed. I had to keep reading.

I looked down at the sword one last time. At that moment I needed to get back to doing what I was supposed to do. Libra would no doubt bring me home when I was done. The Zodians would praise me and ask what I wanted in return. No doubt immediately I would ask for my friends back. Then the four of us would finish finding the rest of the Elders Gems so the earth would stay in tack.

I started walking. I would be able to make it to the house by myself. I would remember the way. I didn't need help. The girls weren't a distraction, they were just… in the way… they were a… obstacle. Obstacles get in the way of what you need to complete. Sometimes you either have to jump over an obstacle or move it out your way. In this case, I would need to move the obstacle out of my way.

When I reached the entrance of the graveyard I tried to remember if I should go left or right… I did need help… with directions. I tried looking to see if there were footprints but got nowhere with that.

I scratched my head and took a chance. "What was that old saying? 'Two lefts make a right' or 'Two rights make a left'? Maybe it was 'Two wrongs make a left'? Yeah! So, I want to go left, but that one's wrong. So, I pick left again and that's another wrong. So, I go right… I get it now!" So, I went right. The thing was… that wasn't right.

Instead of going left I chose right. By the time I realized I went the wrong way, I found out that the saying I used was wrong. The saying goes 'Two wrongs make a right'. So, I should've gone left. To be completely honest, I still don't understand that saying. All I know is that I should've gone left but I went right. Therefore, I was stuck in the woods.

It was still dark out. While I walked through the forest, I heard an owl hooting and a bear growl. When I heard the bear, I started running. Back when I was a boy scout (real boys are boy scouts) I was taught that if a bear has cubs with it and it sees a human, it would attack because it automatically assumes that you're going to hurt its cubs. I also learned how to purify water and build shelter and a bunch of other helpful stuff. Sadly, I'd forgotten how to do all those helpful things.

When I stopped running, I looked up and saw a flock of crows fly above me against the night sky. When they were out of my sight, I heard the bear again only this time it sounded closer. I tried climbing a tree but ultimately failed. By that time the bear sounded as if it were behind me.

When I turned around, I saw two orange eyes glowing through the bushes. I gulped. If I stay really still it can't see me. I thought wrong. It roared and charged out the bushes. I started running as fast as I could even though I knew it was pointless. I was taught that you couldn't out-run a bear. The best thing you could possibly do is pretend to be dead.

I was too scared to try that. The bear was coming up close and that was when I saw something. I saw something fall from the sky. The sword was back somehow. I picked up speed and grabbed the sword from the ground. The brown bear came running up fast and I stabbed it in its forearm, but it didn't fall to the ground.

It roared at me and it backed up. It clenched its forearm, as it stood straight up on its hind legs. Its eyes glowed brighter and it all of a sudden was a bobcat.

I backed up. "Leo? Leo, is that you?"

It began walking circles around me. "Leo it's me... Lancaster." It walked smaller circles around me getting closer to me.

"I'm Aquarius's son."

Even smaller circles.

"Just forget it." I lunged and stabbed him in his side.

He roared and I withdrew. He then changed into a lion. He slashed at the sword and I almost fell back. I slashed at his face and he lost his balance. I lunged at him again and stabbed his eye. He yelled and cut my shirt. I fell to the ground. I looked and saw that his eye was now at the tip of my sword. I sat up and grabbed my bleeding stomach with my free hand. Leo lay in front of me unconscious. It started to rain. I took the eye from the tip of the sword. I laid the sword down and made my way to Leo. When I touched his mane, it fell from his face and covered the ground.

"What?" I asked in confusion.

Then he started transforming again. Only this time, he was a man. A man with brown hair that opened his eyes slowly. He only had his right eye since I took his left eye. His one orange eye then glowed again and fell out. When the eye hit the ground the one in my hand disappeared and an orange item lay in front of me. Leo's Gem.

The man's eye sockets closed and he collapsed again. I remembered that the Elders use human people to do their bidding. Obviously, Leo chose this guy to have his Gem to kill me that way the earth could be destroyed again... I mean I was just guessing. My guessing skills were sometimes off. You could tell by my grades in school.

I stood and picked the Gem up with the sword. It thundered and I looked down at the man. I didn't want to leave him there so I put the sword at my side and held the Gem tight in my hand. It glowed and at a moment my eyes saw everything orange. The glowing stopped and all the colors came back. I now had Leo's Gem.

"Now how does this Gem work?" I focused. "Form of a cheetah!" Nothing. "I'll worry about this later." I picked up the man with a great struggle and started walking to find my way back to the sister's house.

Sooner or later I would find the house and apologize to the girls for any sorrow or trouble I caused them. Hopefully they would understand and help me. Sooner or later I would go home and have a moment to relax and maybe drink a soda or two. Sooner or later. I prayed for sooner.

When I finally made it to the town twelve men stood in my way. They each had two knives and a machete. Their clothes were dirty and mine were no different. After digging up the grave and the fight I was tired and needed to bathe.

Only one was wearing a hat. The hat was like a pirate's hat and since he smelled like saltwater, I assumed he was one.

The man with the hat gave me a half grin. "What are you doing with that man?" He asked me.

"What's with your accent?" I asked him. I didn't want to tell him that the man had the Leo Gem and his eyes fell out after we fought.

He gave me a full grin. "What country you come from depends on your accent. Judging by yours, you're one of us."

"Which would be?"

He cocked his head slightly. "What is that there on your side?" He asked pointing at the sword.

"It's nothing. It's just a cheap piece of plastic." I lied. "Anyway, what country are you from?"

"Mountains."

"Mountains. Yes, I am from there." I lied again.

He slapped my back. "Well then, allow us to assist you with helping this man." He motioned two men. "Take this man to the nearest hospital." He said to them. They took the man and left.

"Uh… thanks." I said.

He slapped my back again. "What's your name kid?"

"Lancaster."

"Well Lancaster, I'm Philip." He slapped my back again. "That thing at your side isn't a cheap piece of plastic. Word spreads fast. That is the sword from the stone. You were able to pull it from the stone. One of our own brothers."

"By brothers you mean metaphorically…"

"Why haven't we seen you in the Mountains if you do live there?"

"I like keeping to myself." My lies wouldn't stop coming.

"What about your clothes?" He said. Him and the others had dirty T-shirts, mud stained jeans, and black bandanas. He was the only one with a blue jean jacket that had torn sleeves.

"I came here about two days ago. I bought these to blend in."

He slapped my back. "I see. Well, Lancaster, we have been waiting for you. Come back to the Mountains with us and the rest of your brothers will praise you."

I thought about it. First the sword came out of nowhere to help me. Then I find a guy that ends up having the Leo Gem. Now these random guys think I'm from the Mountains and they want me to go back with them. Eh, what do I have to lose? I can't die anyway.

"Sure. I don't see why not." I answered. He slapped my back. "Wonderful! Now, let's get you in your proper clothes."

After a long three-day journey in single cab trucks, we finally arrived at Mountains.

Philip supplied me with jeans, a T-shirt, a denim jacket, and brown hiking boots. It was snowing in Mountains just like the book said, but it wasn't freezing. I was a little chilly, but I somehow wasn't freezing. Philip walked me to the tallest mountain in Mountains. French doors lead into Mountains temple. Philip told me that their leader lives in there.

"You're our next leader." He told me with a smile.

I looked at the sword and remembered the real reason I was there. "I can't be the next leader. I'm just passing through."

"What do you mean?" He asked as he opened the doors and led me down the marble hallway.

"Well… you see… I'm not staying here for long."

"But this is your home." He said as his hand grazed the stone statue in the center of the wide hallway.

"Look, it's complicated." I said.

He sat down on the marble flooring and leaned his back against the statue. "Exactly how complicated is it?"

"If I told you you'd think I'm crazy."

"Try me."

I thought about telling him everything. I mean it wouldn't matter anyway. Besides, maybe he was the one I needed to stop. But if that's the case I shouldn't tell him. But if he attacks me, I'm ready. I put my hand on my sword as a just in case. "Do you know about the Zodians?" I asked him.

He laughed to himself and looked down. "You mean the Elders of Zodia, the Sacred Twelve? They used to tell us those stories when we were kids."

"Who told you the stories?"

"The Elders of Mountains. They would tell us about someone causing the earth to be destroyed and two of the Zodian gods had to remake it. But of course, they're not real. Why would you bring them up?"

I nodded to myself. "They are real. I've met all of them. I'm not from Mountains or Grasslands or Desert. I'm from Germany, but I'm not German though. Aquarius is my father. I was sent by Libra to stop someone from destroying the earth again, but I don't know who or where the person is. At first, I thought this was the story of King Arthur, but now I see that it's kind of not. Look, all I'm saying is, I need help finding the person who will destroy the earth before time runs out."

Philip scratched his head and sighed. "You're right Lancaster... I do think you're crazy." He stood. "I think you need to rest up. I'll leave you to it."

"Philip I'm not crazy. The Zodians are real. And so is the rest of my story."

"Get some rest Lancaster. When you're in your right mind I'll show you around Mountains." He walked for the door.

"Philip..."

"Let him leave." A familiar voice said.

I turned around fast and saw Libra. "Libra!" I turned to face Philip. "Philip look its Libra, one of the Zodians!"

Philip turned around slowly. "Where?" He asked without interest.

"Right here!" I said pointing to Libra.

"He does not see me simply because I do not want him to." Libra said to me.

"Why?" I asked him.

"Lancaster you should seriously sleep." Philip told me again. Then he left.

I turned to Libra. "Great, now he thinks I'm even crazier."

"How is your search going?" Libra asked me completely ignoring my comment.

"Not good actually."

Libra held out his hand. "The Gem."

"What, what Gem?"

He pointed at my eyes.

"Oh right, the Gem." I said. "How do I…?"

"Just pull."

I raised my eyebrow before attempting. I slowly started to pull on my eyeballs. I yelled in pain then saw the Gem glisten in my hand. I blinked slowly. "Here."

He held out his hand and the Gem disappeared. "What have you discovered?"

"Well at first I thought this was the story of King Arthur but then I found out it wasn't. By the way, this is the future, right?"

"Why does it matter?" Libra asked me.

"Because I found these eight girls that were a great help to me, until I messed up. Anyway, one of them showed me some books Virgo wrote. Virgo talked about how…" I stopped myself. I had to word this correctly. "How Sofia's mom was killed randomly. Her name was Maria, just like one of the eight girls I met."

"How did Virgo say the woman died?"

What did I just get myself into? "She didn't say exactly. She just said that she was randomly killed."

"When were the books written?"

None of the Zodians knew about her writing the books! No wonder they never told me! "I don't know. I only read that one small, tiny paragraph. Anyway, did you hear my prayer?" I asked trying to change the subject.

"I hear all, yes."

"Is that why you came?"

"No. I came to inform you that the person you are searching for is almost ready to destroy the earth. You must make haste."

"Who's the person? How do I stop them?" I asked sounding more desperate then I was.

"You must figure that out on your own."

"I've been trying to! This would be a lot easier if I had help!"

"You said eight girls were helping you. Where are they now?" He asked.

"I don't know." I grabbed the sword. "I left this thing then got in danger. When I was in danger it fell from the sky and saved me."

"You are smarter than you think you are. You can figure everything out on your own." Libra said confidently.

"Will the sword help me stop the person from destroying the earth?"

"Figure it out."

I sighed. "I can't. I can't stop the person unless I know who it is."

"It seems that you have met quite a lot of people. Perhaps one of them is who you are looking for. Perhaps."

I looked down. "Libra please, please just let me leave. Please let me go home and enjoy my last days on earth."

He said nothing. I looked up and saw why. He was gone. I sighed. "Someone I met is the person I'm looking for... perhaps."

I sat down with my back against the statue and started thinking back to day one. "I met Ector, his wife, and Kay. Then I met the eight girls then, King Eddington, Fredrick and... Pollux!" I heard the bells again. "It's him! How could I have missed it! No wonder I heard bells!"

I jumped up and ran out to find Philip standing there as if waiting for me. "What are you still doing here?" I asked him.

"I knew you wouldn't sleep so I waited for you to come back out. Come on. I'll show you around."

"Who is Louie Eddington?" I asked him.

Philip shook his head. "He was our king."

"Why did he leave?"

He sneaked a woman into Mountains. On top of that, they had a son."

"Named Pollux." The bells.

"Yes. Why does it matter?"

"I already told you why."

"Lancaster…"

I held my hand up. "Mountaineers are good at engineering, correct?"

"Yes."

"I need an airplane."

Philip laughed. "We haven't had a working airplane in seventy years."

"Do you have any prototypes?"

"Lancaster you would be crazy to… yes, we have a helicopter."

"Show me." I wanted an airplane because it would be faster to fly then to walk or go by truck.

Philip quickly took me to the prototype helicopter. It had the outside body of a helicopter, a pilot's seat in the front and co-pilot's seat in the back, and had airplane's wings on the side. The rusty prototype had the word Pterodactyl written on its two sides and wings.

I hopped in the pilot's seat and looked down at Philip. "Get in."

"No way. I am not…"

"I'm your new leader so obey me. Get in." To tell the truth the only reason why I wanted Philip to come with me was because I didn't know how to pilot a plane, especially one like this. I would've let him pilot but I didn't trust him that much.

He hoped in the seat behind me and sighed. "Do you even know how to pilot this thing?"

"Of course, I do." I lied. I'd played video games that had helicopters in it so I imagined this wouldn't be any harder. I was wrong.

"Pull up! Pull up!" Philip yelled into his headset.

I was flying the helicopter just fine until I went up to high. Pterodactyl could only go up 15,000 feet max but apparently, I took it up passed that.

"I'm trying!" I yelled back. I tried to pull the old prototype up but it wasn't working. Don't panic. These are probably ejector seats. "Are these ejector seats?" I asked Philip through my headset.

"No! I told you Pterodactyl is a prototype! We haven't added those yet!"

"Well darn it all!" We had descended to about 9,000 feet and the controls were jamming. I continued to try to pull up but it was no use. I sighed. If only I had the Aquarius Gem.

For some reason I got a crazy, stupid, deadly idea. I unfastened my seat belt and started opening the glass.

"Lancaster what do you think you're doing?!" Philip yelled.

"I don't know! I... I think I'm saving us..." When the glass fully opened, I immediately was flung out of the helicopter.

I was free falling in the air when I realized what I just did. I was falling faster than the helicopter. I turned my body to face the helicopter and saw Philip inside yelling at me but I couldn't make out what he was saying. I cracked my knuckles and exhaled. "Let's hope this works." I formed a triangle with my hands and aimed them at the helicopter.

The helicopter shot up in the air. I laughed. "Holy Zodiac! It worked! I can somehow control metal!" I brought my hands to the prayer position and the helicopter came at me.

I grabbed onto the wing and stood up on it. With one of my hands against the helicopter's side, my other hand was focused on landing me and Philip safely.

When I landed the helicopter in the middle of nowhere Philip exited it. His face turned green and he vomited. "Uh, are you okay Philip?"

When he was finished, he looked up at me. "No! That was the scariest moment of my life! And how did you move the helicopter like that?!"

I put my hand on his shoulder. "I'm not sure. I already told you that I'm Aquarius' son. Maybe that means I have his powers too."

"The Sacred Twelve aren't real!"

"Then how did I do that?"

He sighed. "I don't know."

"How much farther until we reach Grasslands?" I asked him.

"Look around you. We are in Grasslands."

I looked around and saw that he was right. "Looks like I can pilot a helicopter."

"Whatever you say Lancaster. Now can we hurry and find whoever you're looking for?" He asked out of breath.

"I don't see why you're out of breath. I'm the one that moved a helicopter with my bare hands."

Philip and I left the helicopter and walked the rest of the way. We left the forest and found little merchant shops vacated.

"Where are the merchants?" I asked.

Philip shrugged. He looked forward and saw a man walking. "Let's ask him." We walked to the man and he immediately held his head down.

"Yes?" He asked. His voice sounded familiar.

"Where are all the merchants?" Philip asked him.

"I am not sure." The man showed us his face. "Perhaps they are... tied up."

"Hey, I know you." I said to him. "You're the guy that gave me the magic book."

He cocked his head at me. "Yes I am. Did you find it useful?"

"Yeah, why?"

"Just curious. I thought a boy like you would not read such a thing."

"Magic isn't real." Philip said unnecessarily.

The man laughed. "Even the blind can see that magic is what bounds this cursed world." He turned to me. "Isn't that right, Absalom?"

"Absalom? My name isn't..."

"My nieces are very informative." He said walking closer to me. "You cheated your death Absalom. How?"

"Raphael." The name involuntarily came across my lips. "You should be dead."

"How did you cheat your death?" He asked me again with more force.

"Look at me! I'm thirteen, I'm not Absalom!"

"You dabbled in magic yourself. When I first saw you, I knew you looked rather familiar."

"What are you two talking about?!" Philip asked.

"Silence!" Lightning shot from Raphael's fingers tips and hit Philip sending him airborne.

"Philip!" I yelled.

Raphael grabbed me by the shoulders. "We had an agreement. You would give me the Aries Gem so long as your wife escaped her sickness."

I thought out loud. "She didn't."

"Yes, she did! She did and yet you hid the Gem!"

"And you killed me."

"How did you return Absalom?!"

Instead of answering his question I grabbed the sword and stabbed his chest. He yelled and fell to the ground.

I spun the sword around in my hand and put the blade to his throat. "Get up, slowly." I said to him.

"Don't move." A familiar voice said. "Don't move!"

I turned and looked back and saw the eight sisters standing side by side. "Don't move." Maria warned me again.

"You all lied to me." I said feeling betrayed.

"Who hasn't?" Maria said back to me.

That was a good question. But maybe Aquarius and the others didn't lie to me. "Where's Pollux?" I asked.

"Yield or you die." Maria said back to me.

"Wrong answer, I said." I killed Raphael. I chopped his head off and it rolled to Constance's feet. "Okay ladies, Who's next?"

Constance cursed. "You will pay!"

"Where is Pollux!" I asked again loudly.

The eight girls stepped forward and changed. They changed into… creatures? Their skin turned scaly like a snake, their fingers tips grew long and sharp, their feet became claws, their eyes glowed red, and bat wings sprouted from their backs.

I observed them. "So, I'm guessing you're not Sofia's mother. I guess there is more than one Maria in the world."

They did an ear-piercing screech and attacked me in unison. I blocked their attacks one by one easily. I didn't want to continue attacking them back simply because I wasn't after them. I was after Pollux.

But they kept attacking. I lunged back only to cause them to fly into the air. Seeing them fly reminded me of the helicopter. "I needed metal." I looked around fast but saw nothing metal. Then I looked in my hand.

I only looked in my hand and the sword levitated and shot up in the air. It stabbed... whoever in the chest and they fell at my feet. She changed back into her human self and I saw that it was Trinity. I put the sword at my side and picked her up. I ran to find Philip. He was lying unconscious on the ground and I kicked his stomach until his eyes opened.

He looked at me. "I'm going to kill that guy. And stop kicking me!" I was relieved he woke up.

"Don't worry I already killed Raphael. We got to go. Now."

I didn't have to tell him twice. He stood up and with Trinity still in my arms, we started to run immediately. The seven girls just stood and watched us as we got away. I knew that there had to be a good reason why. I didn't see why they would just let us run free. I didn't see why they lied to me like that. Maybe I was Absalom... NO! I was not Absalom! It was just part of their lie. It had to be. It just had to be.

Philip stopped me from running. "Where exactly are we going again?" He asked.

"We need to find Pollux. Fast."

"Well, where exactly is this Pollux?" Philip asked hesitantly.

"I have no idea." I looked at Trinity. "But she might know where he is."

I laid her down gently on the ground. "Is she dead?" I asked looking at Philip for assurance.

"I don't know. Feel her pulse and see." Philip suggested.

I felt her pulse. "She has a pulse but barely. When she wakes up, we can…"

"I thought you said we needed to find Pollux fast." Philip reminded me.

"We do but I have no idea where he could…" I stopped.

"What?" Philip said looking at me strangely.

"Where are the biggest houses?"

"I've only been here a few times, but I think that way." He said pointing. "Why?"

"If we find Pollux's dad, we find Pollux. His dad will be at one of the biggest houses."

"Why? Is he king?"

I smiled. "No. I am king."

With Trinity back in my arms, Philip led me to the biggest houses he knew of. They were ten times bigger than the girls' house. We ran pass them one by one until we saw a parked carriage.

I gave Trinity to Philip. "Stay here until I call you." I told him.

"Got it."

I walked slowly to the parked carriage and saw Fredrick sitting down up against it. "Fredrick I really need your help. I need to know where Pollux is."

No response.

"Fredrick?" I walked closer and saw that his eyes were wide open but he was dead. I knelt beside him and closed his eyes. "Aries take your soul." I looked in the carriage and saw that Louie Eddington was dead also.

I looked around and yelled. "Pollux! Where are you! Stop hiding and face me you coward!"

I looked back at Philip to make sure he was still alive. I motioned him to come to me.

He came running up and looked around. "What?"

"Pollux killed these two. I need to find him before he kills anyone else."

"Too late." A voice said. Pollux slowly walked up. "Louie was still trying to find a house when my protectors told me that you had arrived again. So, I killed Louie, Fredrick, and everyone that lived in these houses. That includes women and children."

"Just because I came?" I asked angrily.

"Yeah. If you would've stayed in Germany this would've never happened. Right now, you would be at home reading all about the Sacred Twelve and how marvelous they are." He laughed.

"Disclaimer: they don't exist." Philip said.

"Philip shut up." I said as I drew the sword. "This ends now Pollux."

He raised his eyebrow. "You plan on killing me?"

"Yes, yes I do."

"If you kill me you die." Pollux said laughing.

"Stop joking around." I told him with a stern look.

"I'm not joking. Think way back when you and your friends were trying to find the Temple of Zodia. Who do you think threw that javelin at you?"

I lowered the sword. "You just said that if I die you die."

"Right. I wanted us to be together again. When you died, I thought that we would go back to our rightful places, but instead somehow Aries got you and let you live again. I tried killing you again but the same thing happened."

"Back up. What do mean you want us to be together and in our right places?"

"Who do you think caused that unusual weather in New York? Mother Nature? No, it was me trying to get you. Think, why would someone want to single handedly destroy the earth?"

"I'm not following your twisted thoughts."

"I did all of this to talk to you."

"What could you possibly tell me?"

"I would tell you what they don't want you to know."

"When you say 'they' do you mean the Elders?"

"Of course, I mean the Elders."

"What do they not want me to know?"

Then Trinity grunted and her eyes opened. She pushed Philip and caused him and herself to fall. She stood up and growled at me.

"Go join your sisters." Pollux commanded her.

"As you wish, my lord." She grew her wings and flew away.

I looked back at Pollux. "What do the Zodians not want me to know?"

"Do I look familiar to you at all? Take a good look."

I thought about the question. "Yeah, somewhat I think, why do you ask?"

He walked to me and I held the sword up. He lowered it and smiled. "There are constellations named after the Zodians. Are you aware of that?"

"Yeah, I am very aware of it. So, what. They each created their own constellations when Libra was making the stars. I read about it in a book."

"The book is correct. The constellation Gemini has only two stars. One is named Pollux the other is…"

"Castor." I said slowly. I dropped the sword and fell on my knees.

Pollux knelt in front of me. "Good to see you again… brother."

Who Is In Control

"There is no way!" I protested. "We are not brothers! You're lying!" I said to him forcefully.

But Pollux attention changed and he turned and looked at Philip. "I don't see why you're still alive. Raphael's attack should've killed you." He took a step closer to Philip. "Who are you?"

Philip looked around nervously. "I'm Philip. I live in Mountains."

"Why are you lying?" Pollux laid his finger on Philip's chest. "Drop dead."

In a cascade of blood and screams Philip hit the ground dead.

"Philip!" I screamed running over to him.

Pollux held me back. "He wasn't who he said he was. He was sent by one of the Zodians to stop me."

"Stop you, stop you from what?" I asked angrily, thinking how I was sent by the Zodians to stop someone also.

He did a smug smile. "The Elders don't want me to tell you the truth."

There was no way I would believe anything Pollux would tell me, but I had to listen. I had to stop him… kill him, but I felt that I had to listen. "What truth?"

"As you said yourself each of the Elders created their own constellations. Gemini only created two stars with hers. She named them Pollux and Castor. Instead of her wasting her time with a mortal man she decided to take the easy route."

I sat on the ground and looked at Philip as I listened. "What easy route?" I asked as if I was interested.

"She was able to learn a spell that greatly assisted her with her plan. Her plan was to mold her two stars into people, babies. She succeeded by creating two baby boys."

I shot up. "You're lying. I'm Aquarius' son."

"Do you really truly believe that?"

I held my head down and remembered what Maria told me in the library, 'you shouldn't believe everything you're told.'

Pollux smiled and laughed. "After we were born Gemini had to hide us from the Zodians."

"Why?"

"She had to make sure none of them knew that we were created by magic and silhouettes. Mostly magic though."

"So, let me get this straight. Gemini created you and me from the stars in her constellations, hid us from the Zodians, and I'm guessing she got tired of hiding us so she just set us on earth to fend for ourselves."

He patted my head. "You're a smart one after all."

I moved his hand from my head. "I don't believe that. I don't believe anything you are saying."

"Well then I guess you won't believe this: all of this you see around you is real. This is the future, although the future can always be altered."

"I know all of this is real. Bottom line is you're the one that's trying to destroy the earth so now I have to kill you." I put the sword to his throat.

"Look around you. Does anything look destroyed?"

"Well... no. But Libra told me to stop you."

He pushed the sword away from his neck. "Libra told you that someone was planning the earth's destruction, right? He was lying. He knew that I really wanted to tell you the truth about everything. So, he lied and told you to kill me to ensure you would never know who you are."

"I want to hear that from them and only them, not you and you alone."

Pollux pointed behind me. "Okay, go ahead and ask them."

Holy Zodiac! When I turned around, I saw all of the Elders standing up in a straight line. None of them looked happy, including Cancer. I dropped the sword. "Hi dad." I said waving to Aquarius.

He ran his hand through his hair. "Did you not hear Pollux's story?"

"What? You all expect me to really believe that Gemini…" Then I stopped and looked at Gemini. "Your constellation still has its two stars, right."

"They're not stars… they're silhouettes used to look like stars." Gemini said slowly.

Cancer shook his head. "All these centuries and I never knew I had two twin nephews." He said quietly. "Sis, why would you…?"

"Don't even ask." Virgo told him. "Obviously she didn't find these two important enough to tell us."

"That's not true! They are important to me." Gemini protested. She looked at Sagittarius for some guidance. "Well now what?" She asked him.

"Well what now?" Pollux asked Sagittarius also.

Sagittarius sighed. "I can't tell now. We have to wait a little longer."

"A little longer for what?" Pollux and I asked simultaneously.

"Kill them." Taurus said. "We shouldn't take a chance, let's just kill them."

"Okay someone better explain what you guys are blabbering about or else... Tell us, what now!" Pollux said in a fiery tone.

"Shut up Pollux." Gemini said.

Libra sighed. "Yes, we tell them now." It was more of a command then a vote. "Centuries ago, Sagittarius, not Aries, foresaw a great malevolent entity with powers that would end all life, including us. That was the very reason we created the Gems; they were a backup source of power for us. As you know Cancer caused the Gems to scatter thus the mortals used them and destroyed the earth... you should know the rest."

"So basically, you're saying that you all think me and Pollux are the malevolent entity Sagittarius was talking about that will destroy all living things. But wait, it was Aries who saw the vision not Sagittarius, right." I asked.

"No, it was not Aries, it was Sagittarius who saw the vision of the malevolent entity. And it is you and Pollux." Libra said sadly.

"And so, because you think that, you're going to listen to what Taurus, mister muscles, says and kill us?" Pollux asked.

"If we do kill them, I don't want them in the After Life." Aries said.

"Of course, I can always make arrangements for them to go to your son Scorpio." Libra said.

"You can't just kill us!" I yelled.

"He's right, you can't kill us. We're immortal." Pollux said with a grin.

"What are you talking about Pollux, I am not immortal. I've died twice before."

Pollux looked at Aries. "Why would you cheat and make him go to the After Life?"

"You cannot cheat death." Aries said back to him.

"Are we killing them or not?!" Taurus asked frustrated.

Pollux did his smug grin. "If you kill us then you have to kill everyone involved in helping me reach Castor. Do you all agree?"

They all got confused looks on their faces.

"Do you all agree?" Pollux asked again.

"No, I do not agree." Taurus said.

Pollux laughed. "Of course, you don't agree Taurus. You don't agree because your daughter helped me."

"What?" Virgo said. "Taurus your daughter helped, is this true?"

"Your children helped too, Virgo." Pollux said pointing at Virgo.

"Children, there is more than just Mercy?" I asked.

"Yes, there is Mercy and Nathaniel." Pollux said as if I should know.

"Nathaniel's your son?!" I asked Virgo.

She rolled her eyes. "Yes, he's my son."

"But… she didn't tell me…"

"Why would I tell you?" Virgo asked.

"Alright hold on a minute." Cancer said. "I just have to ask this question: why are there three dead guys here?"

"Because I killed them." Pollux pointed at Philip. "Which one of you sent this one as a spy?"

They all got quiet. I looked at each one of them as they exchanged looks as if each look was a code. Aquarius nudged Cancer and he looked at Pisces who looked at Leo. Leo's tiger form growled and he stared at Taurus. Taurus scratched his forehead and looked at no one.

Scorpio broke the silence. "Who was it that sent the spy?!" He yelled.

"He was mine." Pisces said. "When I found out Leo's spy was sent to kill Lancaster I sent in Philip. I told Philip to wait for Lancaster and befriend him."

"But he kept saying the Zodians weren't real." I mentioned.

"That was a part of his character." Pisces said.

"Makes sense." Cancer said. "You knew Lancaster could handle the dude Leo threw at him so you told Philip to stay put. But I do have one question for you Lancaster: how did you know you could control the helicopter?"

I backed up. "How do you know about that?" I asked Cancer in a curious voice.

All the Elders snickered.

"I can read minds. Duh." Cancer said boldly.

"Oh, right." I said in a low and slow tone with my head down. "I forget."

"How did you know you could do that?" Aquarius asked me.

"I don't know. I guess I just knew. Why do you ask?"

"Can we please vote to see if we should kill Pollux and Castor?" Taurus asked more agitated now.

"Very well." In the blink of an eye, Libra brought us into the throne room of the Temple of Zodia.

I remembered when they were voting on the same thing as now. I was voted to stay alive, but this time I didn't think the same verdict was going to happen.

Pollux arrogantly yawned. "Can we get on with this?"

I slapped the back of his head. "What's wrong with you?"

He cocked his head and turned to me slowly. "Never ever hit me again."

"I'm not scared of you." I lied.

He straightened his head. "Good." He slapped me with extraordinary power from his hand. His slap made me go airborne through the room's wall and beyond. Each time I went through a wall my headache got worse and worse. I finally landed on the Temple's library floor.

"AH!" I yelled in serious pain.

"You're weaker than I thought." A familiar voice said.

I lifted my blurry gaze. "Sofia?"

"Am I dead?" I asked.

She helped me up and sat me in one of the chairs. She sat in the one beside me. "No. I'm just alive."

"But how are you alive?"

She put her hand on my forehead and smiled. "I expected you to be much stronger by now." Her hands glowed green. "Daddy finally convinced Aries to set me free from the After Life. I told daddy I would only live again if Peter and Judas could live too." The glowing stopped. "Feel better?"

"Yeah, thanks." I didn't bother asking her how she did that simply because what Pollux said about her and Virgo's kids. "So, where're Peter and Judas?"

"I don't know. I decided to stay here for a while. Peter and Judas went their separate ways."

"Did you help Pollux?" I asked. Apparently, everything he said was true, but still I needed to make sure.

She crossed her legs and folded her arms. "He's a bigger idiot than I thought. Why would he tell who helped him?"

"So that's a yes?" I said.

She nodded. "Me, Mercy, and Nathaniel agreed to help Pollux get you and tell you the truth."

"Why you three?"

"He needed magic usurers to help him. We were going to use Lance but he wouldn't do it."

"Wait, so you are a…"

"Yes. I'm a sorceress." She turned her head and that's when I noticed her deep green eyes.

"Were you Maria?"

"Who?" She asked with a frowned face.

"Were you one of the eight girls?"

She thought about the question. "You must be referring to Pollux's guardians. He created them only because he wanted to make sure you were safe until he reached you."

I rubbed my face. "Of course, he wanted me protected." I said sarcastically.

"He tries to be good he just isn't that great at it. Give him some time and he will greatly improve."

"Do the other Zodians know that you, Mercy, and Nathaniel helped Pollux?" I asked just to test her.

"No. And you can't tell them."

"We already know thanks to Pollux." Libra said.

In the blink of an eye the two of us were standing up back in the throne room. Pollux sat on the ground and was attempting to tie his shoes. He glanced at us and looked back down at his shoes. "I thought you were dead Sofia."

Sofia ran and kicked him in the head. "Why the heck was killing me a part of your plan?!" She screamed at Pollux.

Pollux kept his head reared back. "I didn't need you any longer."

Virgo sighed. "And yet you still need Mercy?"

"No, I don't. I only keep her alive because I know how much she means to you." He said mordantly and with a sly smile.

"I vote we kill them." Virgo said immediately. "All in favor say I."

Aquarius shook his head. "Virgo, we are not going to kill them. There are other methods to use."

Gemini looked down. "All of this is my fault."

"Yeah it is." Pollux said giving up on tying his shoes. He stood. "Don't worry though, at least Castor turned out right."

"My name is Lancaster." I corrected. "Right dad?" I asked Aquarius.

He ran his hand through his hair. "I apologize for the lies, Castor."

At that moment my heart burned. I was angry and sad. I wanted to cry and kill at the same time. "So, I'm guessing you lied about Aries being your brother too?"

Aries removed his hood. "You should've stayed in the After Life the first time you came."

Cancer clapper his hands. "Drama!"

Virgo laughed. "This truly is a fantastic day. We finally find Pollux, Lancaster finds out his whole life was a lie, and now Aquarius and Aries are brothers? Truly this is drama!"

"Would someone please tell me our sentence for telling my brother the truth?" Pollux asked annoyed. "I mean come on we can't get in trouble for telling the truth."

Sagittarius stood. "Sofia, which one?"

Pollux and I turned to Sofia. She blinked slowly. I looked at Pollux and he looked as confused as I did.

"Sofia, which one?" Sagittarius asked again.

She blinked rapidly before answering. "I don't know."

"Yes, you do." Cancer said. "I don't even have to read your mind to know that you're lying." He stood and walked toward her. "Just tell us and we'll do the rest. Don't make me have to use my powers."

She backed up and looked at Taurus for help.

Taurus sighed. "Samantha, which one."

Scorpio yelled in exasperation. His trident set on fire and he looked at me and Pollux. "Which one is it?!"

She fell on her knees and put her head in her hands. "Sofia?" I knelt beside her and put my hand on her back. "What are they talking about?"

She lifted her eyes to me. "My lord, I await your orders."

"What?" I asked her.

Cancer nodded his head and looked at his sister. "I'm sorry."

Gemini stood. "Take me instead."

"Just tell me who to burn." Scorpio said to Sagittarius.

Sagittarius stroked his chin. "You won't be burning anyone Scorpio. Gemini, we must do what has to be done."

"Explain now!" I yelled in anger and sorrow.

Sofia grabbed my arm. "You will rule this earth, my lord."

"What about me?" Pollux asked. "I mean I'm the mean and evil one, not Castor."

I ignored Pollux I thought about what Sofia said. I must have been the evil force Sagittarius foresaw centuries ago. I'm the reason why they created the Gems. I guess they didn't know whether the force was me or Pollux so they had Sofia to find out.

"Were we even really friends or did you just befriend me to see if I was the one?"

"My lord I…"

"Stop calling me that. I am not your lord."

"You're right, I am." Pollux said arrogantly. "You are not. Remember that. Now bow to me Sofia."

Sofia rolled her eyes. "My lord, what are your orders?" She asked me again.

"No order matters, Samantha." Taurus stood. "Don't do anything reckless." He said to her.

"My lord, what are your orders?" She asked me again.

"That is, it!" Pollux grabbed me by my shoulders and pushed me on the ground. "Let's be fair with this." He placed his hands on my chest and they started phasing through me.

"Ah!" I screamed in pain. I could feel his hands touching my heart.

My eyes closed and I saw Pollux. He held two swords and he slid one to me. He licked the blade of his sword with his tongue and smiled. "I win I get the power; you win you get the power.

"I'm still confused." I admitted.

He lowered his sword. "Apparently, you're the one that's supposed to take over the world, but I want to take over the world. So, we'll fight for the title."

"But I don't want to."

"You shouldn't be scared brother. I mean don't you want to rule the world?"

"No. Pollux I still don't really understand. I mean, why me?"

"Just shut up and fight." He lunged at me with his sword.

I jumped back and picked up my sword. "This is unnecessary!" I said swinging at his stomach.

He jumped back and smiled. "Come at me bro."

So of course, Pollux was winning the sword battle so far. In my defense swords weren't my strong point. Pollux had me lying on my back and had my sword out of my reach. He held his sword to my throat.

He laughed at me. "Your last words my dear brother?"

I wasn't really in my best condition. My arms and legs had gaping wounds, my bottom lip was cut, and I had a black eye. I could barely even get out the word jerk. Instead it sounded like jek.

He laughed. "I think you mean jerk."

165

I spit on him.

"That's a bold move for a guy in your position." He raised his sword.

Somehow at that moment I remembered what happened with the Pterodactyl. I held up my hands and the sword flew out of his hands.

Pollux stepped back in shock and looked at his hands then me. "That's impossible! You shouldn't be able to do that here!"

I made the swords stab him over and over again until he fell to the ground. I let the swords fall and I knelt beside Pollux.

He lifted his bloody face and stared at me. "Kill me, finish me off."

I shook my head. I didn't want to kill him. I didn't like him but I didn't want to kill him. He was still my brother regardless whether I liked it or not. I stood up and extended my hands to him. He looked at it and smiled. His smile wasn't like all of his other smiles. This was a different smile. This was the kind of smile that warms the heart. He accepted my help and was now on his feet.

"Are you ready to go back for judgment, brother?"

I nodded and we were back in the throne room.

When I looked forward in the throne room everyone was staring at me and Pollux. I noticed that we both weren't bleeding anymore and I now had enough strength to talk.

Sofia ran over to me. "What are your orders-?"

"Don't say my lord." I said to her.

"By the way everyone," Pollux started, "Castor here just won our sword battle. Meaning he is the one to rule the world."

"What do mean by that?" I asked him.

"Yeah I kind of left out a part. Only the true ruler would win that battle. I asked you to kill me because... well... I'm ashamed."

"I'm not ruling anybody! I'm not even strong!" I protested.

"You were able to control metal without the Aquarius Gem. How do you explain that?"

"Well... I..." I didn't have the answer. There was only one answer and I didn't want to say it.

"Well what?" Pollux asked showing his smug smile again.

"Maybe I could do that because I'm Aquarius's son."

Sofia shook her head and looked at the Elders. "What are you going to do?"

"We have no choice but to end his life." Sagittarius said to the other Elders.

"Or trust that what you foresaw centuries ago wasn't me." I suggested.

"It was. We already established that." Pollux said. He walked beside me and whispered, "I have a plan just trust me."

I raised my eyebrow and looked at him. He smiled and faced the Elders. "My brother Castor can't help what he has become and what he will be. So please, spare this poor soul from your cruel wrath."

Cancer shook his head. "Pollux what are planning?"

"Nothing Cancer I'm just trying to save my brother."

Cancer folded his arms. "All of a sudden you want to save your brother?"

"Yeah, I do."

Sofia grabbed my arm. "What are your orders?"

I actually stopped and thought for a second. If Sofia was a magic user that means she could help me get out of the mess I was in. Maybe she could teleport me away from the Temple and then we could find Peter and Judas then think of a plan.

I looked at her. "Teleport me away from here." I whispered.

"Do you have a specific location you would like to go to?" She whispered back.

I thought. "Yes, I do. Take me to Seattle. I want to go to the park where the silhouette catastrophe happened."

"As you wish." She grabbed my arm tight. "What about Pollux?"

I looked and realized his plan. He would be a distraction. I then thought to myself that maybe he wasn't that bad of a guy. "Take him with us."

"As you wish." She glowed then the three of us were in the middle of the park.

I looked around the area and saw the devastation. The grass was now black as if it was burned, all the cars that were parked near the area were now flipped over and crushed, and the playground was now a pile of nothing.

Pollux looked around. "What happened?"

"Years ago, Gemini made silhouettes to find her Gem. When she realized where the Gem was, she forgot all about the silhouettes. The shadows went rogue and destroyed this place." I turned to him. "Is this what will happen to the world?" I asked him.

"It's up to you." He said back to me with a smile.

I picked up one of the apples and remembered the boy up in the tree. He was no older than seven and yet one of the Elders was using him. There is no way that was justified. I killed him but only because he made me mad. He somehow survived and came to me again but Peter shot him with an arrow before he told me who he worked for.

"Deep in thought, brother?" Pollux asked.

I ignored him. Pollux said that it was up to me whether the world would be like that park or not. Wait a minute! I faced the two of them. "Where are all the people who were possessed?"

Pollux turned to Sofia. "Do you know what he's talking about?"

"Yes." Sofia turned to me. "They are no more."

"Explain." I said it in a demanding tone but not on purpose.

"The person leading the silhouettes made them leave the bodies of the people."

"Well who's leading them?" I asked in annoyance. Obviously, she knew I wanted to know.

"Like Virgo said, someone is finding the Zodians weaknesses and using methods to try to kill them. I heard you say that when the silhouette controlled you there was water that you used to defeat the shadow. Think, who would know the Zodians for so long that they would be able to find their weaknesses?"

"I don't have time for this Sofia!" Now I was mad. I needed to know now. "Who is it?!"

Sofia smiled. It was worse than a smile that Pollux would give a person. It was a bone chilling smile that would cause a child to cry and scare grown men. That smile made me realize who the person was.

"Sofia... it's you." I said in shock.

She nodded and her smile grew bigger.

"Why?" I asked.

She pointed to Pollux. "He needed my help so I helped him by trying to find the Elders weaknesses."

"So, you knew about this then?" I asked Pollux.

"No." He said. I could tell by the look in his eyes that he was being honest. "I asked her to help me but I didn't tell her to find the Elders weaknesses. I'm glad she did find them though."

Where to Go

"Sofia, do you know how much trouble you could get in?!" I asked still in shock. I thought someone like Pollux or Judas would do something like that but not someone like Sofia.

"I'll be fine." She said in a reassuring tone.

"How did you do it?" I wanted to know.

She smiled and rolled her eyes. "I'm a witch."

I didn't respond. The fact that she was a witch kind of made sense to me. I mean when we were back in school, she always stuck out. She didn't just stick out because of her eyes though. To be honest there were times when I would be scared of her even though we were best friends. Whenever I got around her, I felt safe and something else. That something else was hard to explain until now. I not only felt protected but also power. I know it sounds weird but it's true. I felt stronger and more confident around her.

"Where are the people and silhouettes?" I asked her.

"The people are collapsed all over the city and the silhouettes are gone." She said smiling.

"As in gone forever, right?" Pollux asked taking my question.

"Yes. They left the apples but inhabited bodies. When I told the silhouettes to leave the bodies they disintegrated."

"Well thank the Zodian gods." Pollux said. "I would hate for one of them to control me."

"Shut up Pollux." I said to him. It was a mean and rather random comment but I needed to think.

Sofia was trying to find the Zodians weaknesses. I needed to ensure that they never found out that it was Sofia. Also, I wanted Pollux dead and everything to go back to normal. By normal I mean me being back at Garamond. By normal I mean Judas giving me a black eye and a bloody nose daily. By normal I mean Sofia saving me half the time when Judas, the bully, would beat me up.

I looked at Pollux. "Who is stronger, me or you?"

He licked his lips. "Who won the battle?"

That answered my question. I thought about killing Pollux right then and there, but Sofia shot me a look that made me think twice. She knew why I asked, obviously, but I wanted/needed Pollux dead. If he didn't die then he might have caused me trouble in the future. Plus, even though I somehow still had Aquarius's powers I wasn't sure the power was still there.

"Why do you ask who is stronger?" He asked me.

"Let's just go." I said ignoring his question.

"Where to?" He responded. He knew not to wonder why his question was unanswered.

My memory then brought me back to Nathaniel and the places he took me. "Sofia."

She looked up at me. "Yes?"

"Take us to Witch Greta." I ordered. This time I meant to sound demanding for more than one reason.

"As you wish." She formed a crimson circle around the three of us and we were then standing in front of an old run-down shack.

I nodded at the sight. It seemed like yesterday I was at that place. I remembered the snakes well. They all greeted me with a hiss then resumed their business.

I looked at Pollux who was holding a viper. I sighed at the sight. "Pollux, you stay here. Sofia, you come with me."

Pollux stroked the snakes head and laughed. "Look at you. You sound like a leader already." He said to me.

"Shut up." I walked to the shack with Sofia behind me.

"Why are we here?" She asked.

"You'll see." I said knocking on the broken door.

The same old, haggish figure as before answered the door. She looked the same except she was wearing a red robe (just like Nathaniel showed me).

She did her witchy laugh and revealed her yellow teeth to us. "What brings you two here?"

"I don't know. Why are we here Castor?" Sofia asked.

"C-c-Castor?" The witch stuttered. "Is that what you called him?"

I started to ask why she seemed so afraid but I didn't care. As long as she would help me, I didn't care if she feared me or not.

"I need you to read me my future." I said to her.

She nodded quickly and gestured Sofia and I to enter. Before I walked in, I looked behind me to see if Pollux was still there. He was sitting on the ground playing with snakes as they came to him.

I entered the shack and everything was the same. The only difference was the table that used to have her magic orb was now fixed and had a purple table cloth over it. Sofia took a seat on the floor but I remained standing. I looked around the small room and then realized that there were two hallways leading out of the room. Somehow the hallways didn't affect the size of the shack on the outside. I knew Witch Greta lived there but I had no idea it was like a house. I thought it was just that one small room.

I looked at Witch Greta. "Hurry up." I said impatiently.

She dragged her crippled green finger on a row of books before responding to my demand. "Of course." She pulled a book off the shelf. "Here it is."

"Well, what's my future?" I asked immediately.

"Gather around children."

I rolled my eyes and walked to the table. Sofia only joined me when I looked at her. I guess she thought she needed my permission even though she didn't.

Witch Greta inhaled and opened the book. A burst of bright light blinded the three of us and I saw something I did not like at all.

I saw me. Only I wasn't... me. I was dressed in black armor and wore a red cape. I was sitting on a golden throne and had the sword I pulled from the stone laying on my right thigh. On my head was tattooed CASTOR and the T looked like a cross. Then Sofia came into view and she bowed before me. She was dressed like a Gothic princess and held a crown in her hands.

My hand motioned for her to stand and she obeyed. She then walked behind me and placed the golden crown on my head. I then saw Gems creatively decorated on the crown. Those Gems weren't like other gems. They were the Zodians Gems. She then walked back in front of me and bowed then I dismissed her. When she was gone, I stood and held the sword in my hand. On both sides of the sword's blade was written JUSTICE. I smiled and nodded.

"Your future." Witch Greta's voice caused the illusion to fade away.

I wiped my eyes and shook my head. "The future can be altered." I informed her.

"Do you really believe that you can alter your future?" She asked intrigued.

I put my head in my hands and sighed. "Sofia we're leaving."

She stood there motionless.

"I said we're leaving." I said with a more demanding tone.

She just stood there wide-eyed as if she didn't hear me.

"Let's go!" I yelled.

She blinked slowly. "You cannot alter what has been written."

"What?"

"Show him." She said to Witch Greta.

The witch pulled back a book from the shelf and the shelf moved to the side to reveal a staircase going down.

Sofia grabbed my arm. "Please, let me show you." She said whispering in my ear.

I nodded. Whatever it was I needed to see it.

Witch Greta handed Sofia a torch.

Sofia looked at me. Arm in arm we walked down the stairs. The bookshelf moved back to its place so only the torch gave us light.

The winding stairs creaked as we descended. I could hear rats squeaking and saw cobwebs with insects that had not been eaten yet.

"Where are you taking me?" I finally asked.

"I'm going to show you your destiny."

I didn't say another word. I didn't need to. She gave me a straight answer and I wanted to see my destiny for myself.

Finally, the stairs ended and Sofia separated herself from me. She pointed at the wall straight in front of us. She gave me the torch and walked to the wall.

Drawn in the stone wall was Gemini's constellation. One star was marked Castor and the other Pollux. A picture of two babies in a woman's arm was drawn beside the constellation. Beside that picture was a teenage boy holding a sword and another teenage boy lay at his feet dead. The boy with the sword had CASTOR written on his head and the other boy had POLLUX written on his head.

I turned to Sofia. "This doesn't mean anything."

"Please accept the fact that this is your destiny."

"Sofia anyone could have drawn these pictures." I said in angry voice.

"Who else do you think knows about this place?" She said back to me in an angrier voice.

"You, Witch Greta, maybe Mercy…"

"No." She shook her head. "You heard it straight from Gemini herself. Gemini is you and Pollux's mother and if you look at the last picture you can see that…"

"That's enough!" I said cutting her off.

"You can't change your destiny." Sofia said to me.

"Watch me." I said to her in a strong commanding voice.

I handed her the torch and walked up the stairs in complete darkness. When I reached the top, the shelf slid to the side and I stepped back into the room. I looked around for Witch Greta.

"Witch Greta!" I yelled. She came wobbling from one of the hallways.

"I do believe you are not happy with what you saw."

"None of it is real." I said.

Sofia passed by me and handed Witch Greta the torch. Witch Greta blew it out and set it on the table. "You two are welcome to stay the night if you like."

"No thanks." I responded. "Come on Sofia let's get Pollux and go, we have to get back."

"Wait a moment." The witch said to me. "There was a boy who came in here only a few moments ago. He wanted me to tell you that he was tired of waiting so he left."

"He left, to go where?" I asked not shocked.

"He didn't say, but I myself did see him teleport away."

I stopped and thought. With Pollux gone I didn't have to worry about any problems. I would stay the night at Witch Greta's house, but not really. When she would fall asleep, I would steal all of her magical items and get Sofia to teleport us away without a trace. Maybe somewhere in Witch Greta's books she had something that could help me change my future.

"You needn't steal my belongings. You can read and use whatever you want. Not that any of it will help you." Witch Greta read my mind. She gestured to one of the hallways. "Your rooms are at the very end of this hallway. I will call you for dinner shortly." She went down the opposite hallway she pointed to.

I looked at Sofia. "It looks like we are staying here for the night."

She folded her arms. "You're not demanding this time?" Her tone sounded playful.

"I am no tyrant." I responded.

"Not yet." She turned and left my sight. I opened the door to the room I was supposed to be staying in. The room smelled like musk and death. Although the room didn't smell to well the actual room itself was okay. I expected cobwebs and spiders everywhere but thank goodness I was wrong.

The bed in the far-left corner was covered in a simple light blue sheet accompanied by two plush pillows. In the far-right corner was a mahogany desk with a wobbly chair placed perfectly in front of it. Beside the closet door was a tiny dresser with broken handles. The room still needed to be upgraded a bit but it would do.

I shut the door and removed my shoes before lying on the bed. I stared at the blank white walls and the recently dusted ceiling fan. I closed my eyes and tried to sleep but I couldn't. How could I sleep? I was just showed a wall that was supposed to be my pass and future, not to mention I was shown my future self.

I sat up and shook my head. There had to somehow be a way I could change the future. Like Nathaniel told me, the future can be altered. He showed me Sofia crying to Witch Greta and Judas with blonde hair and blue eyes. Plus, apparently Sofia killed someone. Was that person me?

I heard a knock on the door and then it opened. Sofia stepped in and gave me a small grin. "Dinner is ready."

"I'm not hungry." I said laying back down.

She shook her head. "Why are you so upset about your future?"

I sat back up fast. "Um… well let's see… I don't know! Maybe I'm upset because I don't want to rule the world! I want to be a normal person!" I yelled.

She looked down. "You'll come around sooner or later."

"Oh, so you want me to rule the world then?"

She gave me a full smile. "Dinner will be waiting for you when you're ready."

"I'm not eating."

She left. I put my face in my hands and sighed. "Please let this all be a dream." I prayed to no particular Zodian. It didn't matter who I prayed to anyway. I lay back down and closed my eyes. I was going to have a good night sleep one way or another.

I was almost asleep when I heard a loud unpleasant noise. I jumped out of bed and scanned the room. I heard the noise again and realized that the noise was my stomach.

"Why didn't I eat dinner?" I asked myself. I slipped my shoes on and quietly opened the door. I shut it behind me and tiptoed down the hall. When I made it to the kitchen, I saw a plate of food sitting on the dinner table. I picked up the plate and was about to make my way back into my room when the lights turned on.

"You should learn to be quieter child." Witch Greta said.

"I thought I was being quiet." I murmured under my breath.

"Have a seat." She said gesturing to one of the four chairs around the table.

I sat down and looked at the plate. The plate had a little macaroni and cheese, some asparagus, and a chocolate chip cookie. I wondered if all witches cooked like that.

"What's troubling you child?" She finally asked.

"What do you think?" I said picking up the fork on the table.

"Is it about your future?" She said taking the seat in front of me.

I ate some macaroni before answering. "Of course, it is."

"You'll come around sooner or later." Witch Greta said.

"Funny, that's what Sofia said." I informed her.

"She's a good girl. Not to mention she's saved you a lot of times."

"Can we please discuss my future instead of my pass?" I took a bite of asparagus.

"What more do want to know about your future?"

"I want to know how to change it."

She cackled. "You cannot change that."

I put down the vegetable. "Not unless I die." I looked up at her awaiting her response.

"Have you ever tried to kill yourself?"

"I've died more than once before Witch Greta."

"And you've always come back."

I carefully thought about my response to that comment. "Explain."

"You explain. You're the one that was there. Explain to me what happened."

Darn it! I responded the wrong way. I honestly thought about it though. Maybe Aries said that he brought me back just to cover up the fact that I was immortal. Maybe that was true, regardless I wasn't going to say anything to Witch Greta.

I stood up. "I'm done here."

I walked to the room Sofia was staying in. I knocked on the door repeatedly until she finally decided to answer.

She scratched her head and rubbed her eyes. "Castor do you know how late it is?"

"We're leaving, let's go." I said.

I only had to say it once. She stepped out of the room and followed me to the bookshelf. I began taking the books without even looking at what they said. I handed half the stack of books to Sofia.

"Teleport us to Pollux."

"I would but I don't know where he is." Sofia said.

"Okay then. Teleport us home."

"Home?" She asked confused.

"Take us back to Calisto. Take us to my house."

She nodded. A green circle surrounded us then we were standing in front of my house. I smiled at the sight. I grabbed the spare key from under the mat and opened the door. I walked up the stairs to my room and threw the books on my unmade bed.

My room was exactly the same as how I left it that day. I breathed in and smiled again. I was finally home.

Sofia looked around my room. "This room is messy."

"It's just the way I left it the day we set out to find the Temple of Zodia."

She nodded. "So why did you take all of these books from Witch Greta?" She said setting her stack on the bed with the others.

"Because there has to be a spell to help me."

"Why do you want to change your future? I honestly don't understand."

"I wouldn't expect you to understand. Now are you going to help me or not?"

She didn't answer. She sat in the chair at my desk and stayed quiet the whole time I was flipping through the books.

After about thirty straight minutes of searching, I grew tired. I rubbed my eyes and glanced at Sofia. I saw that she made herself occupied with reading my books about the Zodians.

She caught sight of me looking and closed the book. "You look tired." She said to me.

"I am, I am very tired."

She stood up and stretched. "You should rest."

"So, should you. There's a room down the hall to the right that you can stay in."

She nodded. "Sleep well."

"Hopefully I will."

A New Beginning

Of course, I didn't sleep well. I kept dreaming about the image of me with the sword and crown. Every time I closed my eyes, I saw myself like that and I kept saying, "Power and justice shall prevail." Each time I heard that phrase the hair on the back of my neck stood on end and I got chills up and down my back.

Finally, I decided to stop trying to sleep. So, dressed in Teenage Mutant Ninja Turtle pajama pants and a fainted blue T-shirt, I put on a black hoodie, grabbed the spare key to the house, secured it in my jacket pocket, and then left the house to go walking around.

Back when everything was normal, I would occasionally walk around outside when I couldn't sleep. Peter had put a stop to that after mom and dad died though. I left out the house and started walking the route I used to walk. I would walk pass the bus stop all the way to the park and back home. All together it would take me about forty minutes to get from the park and back home. When I made it to the bus stop, I rested on the bench like I always did. I would stay there for about five minutes then I would keep walking. While I was resting, I saw four guys walking up to me.

"Oh no." I said quietly to myself.

The four guys stood in front of me.

One of them laughed. "What's a little boy like you doing out here without their mommy?" He sounded like Kay, but he was clearly not Kay.

I ignored him. I didn't want to fight them.

"What's wrong with you kid?" One of the other boys asked with the same accent.

I didn't move or say anything.

"Okay maybe this'll get you talking?" Another said pulling out a gun.

I looked up at the gun. "Please shoot me." I begged the guy. I wasn't kidding either. I wanted to see if I would die. If I did then Aires wouldn't let me return to earth so therefore my future would be no more.

The four of them looked at me confused then they all started laughing. I looked at them. "I'm not kidding. I really want you to shoot me. I dare you."

The guy with the gun nodded. "Alright then, any last words?" He asked putting the gun to my forehead.

At that moment I involuntarily said, "Death is my ally."

He pulled the trigger.

"What the-" The four of them stood back.

I looked up and felt my forehead. There was no blood but the bullet was halfway in my head and I couldn't even feel it. Then I remembered what happened with the Pterodactyl. I was able to control the plane so why wouldn't I be able to control the bullet?

I pulled the bullet from my head and set it on the bench. I stood up. "Thanks for trying." I said to them and I continued my walk.

Was it really that hard for me to die again? I then started thinking about ways to kill myself. Okay, I know how it sounds but I really wanted to die.

"You shouldn't play with death."

I turned around fast. I then saw Aires holding his scythe and tapping his foot. I rubbed my forehead. "You stopped the bullet?" There was no mark where the bullet was.

"You did and you know how. I am just simply saying that death doesn't enjoy those that abuse it."

"You're making it sound like death is a person." I said to him.

He nodded his head. "I am death."

"Why didn't you just up and say that instead of referring to yourself in third person?" I asked.

"My point is, stop messing with death. It is nothing to play with. With death come consequences."

"I want… need to die." I finally said to him.

"Did you not hear what I just said?" Aries said back to me impatiently.

"So, you're not going to let me die?" I looked at Aries in disappointment.

"Why do you even want death to come upon you?"

"You know what, forget it." I put on my hood. "Just leave me alone. Go away Aries-Death."

"As you wish, my lord."

"You're what?" I asked reaching out to touch him. When I touched his robe, he wasn't there anymore. "Oh no. I'm so tired I think I'm starting to hallucinate!" I started running back to the house. If I didn't hurry and sleep who knows what else I would see.

When I made it back up to the bus stop, I saw Sofia sitting on the bench. When I saw her, I stopped. "Are you another hallucination?" I asked her. She cocked her head to the side in confusion.

"Never mind, why are you here?"

She stood up. "I came out looking for you. I came to check on you in your room and you were gone."

"Well I'm fine can we go back home now?" I said sounding really exhausted.

"Why?" Sofia said.

I looked around quickly. "Because…" Suddenly she was gone, there was no one there. I rubbed my eyes. "I got to get some sleep fast."

"Yes, you do, you look terrible. Then again, not everyone can be blessed with my looks."

It was a familiar voice but not really. "Virgo is that really you?"

She nodded. "Who else could I be?"

I stuck my finger out to poke her.

She back away in discuss. "What are you doing?"

"Are you real or a hallucination?"

"Is that a trick question? I think you know the answer."

"Hallucination, right!" She faded away.

"Darn it all!" I pinched myself to ensure I wasn't dreaming. I definitely wasn't, I was just seeing things. My fatigue came on stronger and so it was harder for me to walk home. At times I would have to slap myself in order to stay awake.

Finally, I made it home. I pulled the key out of my pocket and with shaky hands I tried my best to stick it in the keyhole.

"Why are you shaking?" I heard Pollux voice.

I banged my head up against the door. "Great, now I'm hallucinating about Pollux." I said to myself.

"Hallucinating? What do you mean by hallucinating?" He asked.

I turned around and slapped him as hard as I could.

"What did you do that for?!" He yelled as he held the side of his face.

"I'm so sorry!" I yelled taking off my hood.

"I bet you are sorry!"

"No, I really am. I'm just really tired and I've been seeing all of these hallucinations and I thought you were one."

"Well you thought wrong!"

"Why are you here anyway?" I asked trying to change the subject.

"When I left the old shack, I teleported myself to a fast-food place since I was starving. Since I didn't have any money I decided to go back to the shack. When I got back, I heard you tell Sofia to take you home to Calisto so I followed you guys here." He said as he continued to rub his face.

"That doesn't make any sense. Why didn't you just conjure up money?"

He smiled in embarrassment. "I didn't think of that. Anyway, can I crash here for the night… or possibly longer?"

"Fine, you can sleep on the couch." I didn't want him anywhere else in the house.

"Thanks." He took the key from me and opened the door.

I gave Pollux a blanket and a pillow and he relaxed himself on the couch. I made my way up the stairs the best I could and then returned to my room. I threw my hoodie somewhere on the floor and jumped onto my bed. I closed my eyes still seeing that same image of myself, only this time instead of saying the power and justice I was saying, "Behold, for I am the bringer of death."

When morning came, I realized that I probably got maybe two hours of sleep. The sun shined through my window and I shook my head to wake myself up. I stood and walked to the window and saw that Calisto hadn't changed a bit. Everyone was still doing what they were doing before. The only difference I saw was a building that was taller than any other building in the town. I decided that I would go and see what the new building was. Maybe I would even go and check out Garamond and Calibri.

I put on a pair of ripped jeans, applied deodorant, and put on a Dallas Cowboys T-shirt (I was still tired and I didn't feel like showering). I hopped down the stairs to the kitchen to find Sofia and Pollux. Sofia had Pollux pinned up against the counter as she held a knife to his throat.

I shook my head. "Come on Sofia leave him alone."

She looked at me through the corner of her eyes. "Did you invite him in?"

Without waiting for me to answer Pollux loudly said "Yes! I keep telling you that!"

"I didn't ask you; I am asking him." Sofia said putting the knife closer.

"Yes, I let him come in for the night." I said to Sofia.

She threw the knife on the ground and sighed. "How did you sleep?" She asked as if nothing happened.

I picked up the knife and put it back in the drawer. "I got maybe two hours of sleep."

"Well that's not good." Pollux said.

"I know but I'll be fine. I would like for us to go to a few places though." I said.

They both nodded.

"Just let me borrow some of your clothes though." Pollux made his way to my room.

I looked at Sofia. "I don't have any clothes for you, sorry."

"It would have been nice to know you let him stay the night." She said angrily.

"Maybe you can go to your house and change your clothes. Then we all can leave." I said not wanting to get on the subject about Pollux. Sofia didn't like Pollux simply because he left her to die. I didn't blame her for hating him. Still, she needed to learn to get over it.

"As you wish. I'll be back." She left the house but not before cursing under her breath.

When Sofia got back, we left and our first stop was Garamond and Calibri. The schools didn't change. They were still side by side, Garamond still needed to cut their grass and Calibri still had the rich kids.

As soon as I climbed up Garamond's steps and opened the doors memories started flooding back. Some of the memories were good some bad. Regardless I enjoyed reminiscing on them all.

"Whoa check it out! Zodiac Kid has returned!" One of the kids joked. Everyone in the hallway laughed, including Pollux.

"Zodiac Kid?" Pollux asked. "That's kind of funny." He said continuing to laugh.

Sofia punched his arm and looked at me. "Doesn't this place bring back memories?"

"Yep, it sure does." Looking through all the laughing kids I saw a man that made me back up.

Mr. Daster came briskly walking toward me. I turned to Sofia. "Sofia, Mr. Daster's coming." I informed her.

She put her hand up to her head and sighed. "No doubt he has questions about the principal's office incident."

"Wait what's going on?" Pollux asked completely clueless.

"Just stay quiet Pollux." Sofia and I said to him simultaneously.

He zipped his lips and threw away the key.

"Mr. Cyrus O'Hara and Miss Sofia Ferguson, long time no see." Mr. Daster said with a grimace expression.

"Not long enough." Sofia murmured.

"I heard that Miss Ferguson." He looked at Pollux. "Well I see you brought a new friend to help you wreak havoc on this institution."

"I'm looking for Mr. Cazzner." I said.

"Mr. Cazzner is dead." Mr. Daster said quietly. "You, Miss Ferguson, and Mr. Vince are wanted for questioning."

"We didn't kill him." Sofia said knowing that he wouldn't believe that statement.

"Tell that to the local authorities." Mr. Daster looked at Pollux again. "Perhaps he was one of those creatures in the room while you all were killing Mr. Cazzner."

"Yes!" Sofia said quickly. "It was his fault!" She said pointing at him.

"Sofia." I said as a warning.

"Castor let's just admit that Pollux killed Mr. Cazzner." She said slowly.

I knew she had a plan but still I didn't like where it was going.

"Castor?" Mr. Daster asked. "Pollux? Aren't Castor and Pollux the stars in the constellation Gemini? Don't tell me, Mr. O'Hara, that your real name is Castor and that this is your brother." Mr. Daster taught Astrology so of course he knew about the stars that were Castor and Pollux.

"Wow. You catch on fast. What class do you teach?" Pollux asked interested.

Sofia punched him again. "Castor, tell me why we're here again."

"Mr. Daster, you're telling me that Mr. Cazzner is dead, right?" I asked him to make sure.

"Right and you are wanted therefore the police is here right now." He pointed outside. "I called them myself when I heard you were here." He boasted.

Pollux shook his head. "I got this."

"Don't." I told him. "We'll just have to be on the run again."

"So, what do we do?" Sofia asked folding her arms. "You want us to turn ourselves in?"

I scratched my head and looked to see that everyone in the hallway was now staring at us. I didn't want to fight my way out of this mess… then again, there was no other way. Plus, there was a possibility that I could die out there and I still wanted to die.

"Stay here." I commanded Sofia and Pollux.

I opened the doors and the officers immediately drew their weapons. I rolled my eyes.

"Put your hands behind your head!" An officer with the megaphone yelled. "I won't tell you twice!"

I didn't need my hands anyway. I put my hands behind my head and smiled. The cars flew into the air and all the men looked around like idiots. I laughed and sighed. "Now for their guns."

Their guns flew from their hands and turned ready to shoot at all of them.

I felt Sofia touch my shoulder then she whispered, "Do it my lord."

I smiled. "Behold, for I am the bringer of death." I blinked and the guns fired simultaneously. All of the officers fell bloody and Mr. Daster ran pass me and looked at the quick and spectacular work I did.

"What are you?" He asked in fear more than curiosity.

"He's your lord, so bow to him." Pollux said.

All of the kids in school started screaming and running around everywhere.

Mr. Daster pulled out his phone.

"Mr. Daster, look up." I directed his attention to the police car dangling above him.

He fell on the ground in fear. "Please don't kill me. Please!"

Pollux picked Mr. Daster up by his bow tie. "Stop begging." Pollux turned to me. "Can I do the honor?" He asked.

"Do whatever you want to do to him and these two schools." I said. "Sofia, there's a new building here and I want to see what it is. You're coming with me." I instructed her.

"Yes, my lord." Sofia said respectfully.

Turns out the new building was a new police station. I personally didn't understand why it was the tallest building in Calisto, but I really didn't care why. So anyway, when Sofia and I walked inside we saw pictures of us and Judas on wanted posters. They were looking for us for a while apparently. Of course, the officer's downstairs threatened to shoot us if we didn't do as they said, so I used their own weapons to shoot them.

By the time Sofia and I got back home Pollux was sitting outside the door waiting.

"Finally, I've been waiting forever now." He said.

I put my hands in my pockets. "I don't have the key so…" I cocked my head and the door unlocked. I smiled. By now I pretty much mastered my magnetism powers and I didn't even need the Gem.

Pollux walked in but Sofia closed the door before me and she could enter. She smiled at me.

"What?" I asked.

"I knew you would come around."

"What are you talking about?" I said sitting at the doorstep.

"You talked all about how you hated your destiny, and yet now you're embracing it. I'm glad you finally decided to come around."

I wiped my face with my hand. She was right. I just full out killed innocent people and no doubt the police would definitely be after us even more. All of these things were facts. I didn't care though. That was the biggest problem and fact of all.

She sat beside me. "Just before you killed the officers you said, 'Behold, for I am the bringer of death.'"

"When will I rule the world?" I didn't want to believe whatever her answer was, but I still asked.

"I'm not sure."

"Why did you tell me to kill them?"

She stood up and brushed herself off. "You would've done it anyway, so I told you to kill them." She off walked in the house.

I stood up. The Zodian gods knew that I tried my best to not follow my destiny. No one even wanted to stop me. I needed help. I needed Aries.

"Aries!" I started to yell. "Aries, take me to the After Life! Aries, I need to talk to you now! Let me go back to the After Life!"

Everyone walking by the house started staring and pointing. They were acting like I was mental and by the looks of it some of them heard about the shooting at the school. I shook my head. "Aries, if you don't take me, I'll take them!" My hands glowed green and I screamed in pain. I saw a hooded figure in front of me and then I was right where I wanted to be, with Aries in the After Life.

"What has gotten into you?!" Aries asked as he sat in his office chair. He had taken us back to his office in the After Life.

I sat in one of chairs in front of his desk. "You know my destiny." I said to him.

"And you pick now to embrace it?" He asked me.

"Well I have to accept it someday, right."

He shook his head. "Just today you have slain forty-seven innocent people. You are filling the After Life unnecessarily!"

"Well I don't see a problem? I'm sure they all picked the paradise side of this place anyway. You've told me how the After-Life works."

He shook his head and removed his hood. "You were naive when I told you how this place works. Needless to say, I lied to you. You cannot choose your afterlife. I determine that. I decide by the life the person lived on earth and their death."

"So, if a person was a murderer who was killed by police officers trying to stop him…"

"Paradise is not the murderer's home." He said finishing my sentence.

I leaned back in the chair and sighed. "Just put me on the side where the murderers go."

"Oh, trust me I would, but even if I did you would escape."

"How would I escape?"

"You know your destiny. You will be all-powerful therefore it will be easy for you to escape death."

"Makes sense, I guess. So, what now I just wait to snap again and do more killings?" I asked unsure of his answer.

"It's your choice." Aries said to me.

I stood up. "'Behold, for I am the bringer of death.' 'Power and justice shall prevail.' From what I can see, I will have power but not justice."

"Perhaps that is more of a fact than an opinion." Aries offered.

I wasn't offended. It was true. Maybe. "Can you take me back now?"

"Of course." He stood up but with a great struggle. His back cracked repeatedly before he stood up straight.

I looked at him in shock. It was strange for me to see an all-powerful god have scoliosis. "Are you okay?"

"I'm fine." He said as if it were painful to speak. I grabbed his scythe for him and sighed. "Hold still he said."

"Thank you. Thank you for all the help you've given me in the pass and present." I said genuinely.

He nodded. He skillfully twirled his scythe and then threw it like a javelin. The blade hit me and I blinked hard. When my eyes opened, I was laying on my couch in my house.

I sat up fast to see Sofia sitting on the carpet waiting for me to wake up. I looked around. "How did I get here?"

"I found you outside and Pollux carried you in and set you on the couch. I've been waiting for you to come back."

"What do you mean come back?" I asked standing up.

"Only your spirit left you, your physical body was still here with us."

I nodded in understanding. "Before Aries took me my hands glowed green. Why is that?"

She stood. "If you're going to rule the universe you have to have more than the power of magnetism."

"I want to go to the Temple of Zodia." I said at random. I remembered what Daster said. Apparently Cazzner was dead, but I needed to ask the guy that made him into Azznic.

"Road trip!" Pollux yelled out of nowhere. He appeared in my sight. "Let's go." He said with a big smile.

"You can come if you take us there." Sofia said to him.

"All aboard to the Temple of Zodia!"

"Just shut up and take us there." I warned.

He saluted me. "Yes, my lord!"

After Pollux teleported us to the Temple, we walked to the throne room to find Sagittarius playing his wooden flute and Virgo playing the harp. The music was pretty and mesmerizing but it ended when Virgo saw us.

She rolled her eyes. "What are you three doing here?"

Sagittarius continued to play.

"Where is Aquarius?" I asked.

"I don't know go ask someone else." She said about to resume playing.

"Where is everyone else?" I asked getting annoyed.

She ignored me and began playing again.

I rolled my eyes. "Come on." I commanded Sofia and Pollux.

The three of us wandered aimlessly through the Temple. We found the pool and saw Pisces playing with the dolphins. He waved at us. "Hello! What brings you three here again?"

I liked Pisces. He was never rude to me and he was always happy. "We're looking for Aquarius." I told him returning his smile.

He petted one of the dolphin's head. "I can't say I've seen him. Check the kitchen or maybe the gym even."

I thanked him and again we walked down endless hallways after hallways. We found the kitchen where Cancer was making himself a sandwich. He did a double take when he saw us. "What are you three doing here?" He squeezed way too much mustard over his bread.

"Have you seen Aquarius?" Sofia said.

Cancer lazily laid roast beef on top of the mustard. "What if I have?"

"Then I strongly suggest you tell us." I said walking closer to him.

He looked at me through the corner of his eye as he added Swiss cheese to his sandwich. "I'm a god. You don't scare me."

"Obviously you're not the smartest god." Pollux said under his breath.

Cancer over did the mustard again. "Get out of the Temple."

"Make me." I said folding my arms.

"If you say so." When he placed the top bread on his sandwich I started levitating in the air. He looked at me. "Would you like for me to blast you through the doors?"

"Do it. Prove that you're stronger than me." I challenged.

Cancer sighed and I was back on the ground. He picked up his sandwich and got a napkin. "Aquarius and Gemini left about an hour ago. I'm not sure where they went but they might be back soon." He left with his sandwich and a glass of water.

"Question: why do we need to talk to Aquarius?" Pollux asked leaning up against the wall.

"Sofia, go find Aquarius and Gemini. When you find them separate Gemini from Aquarius and keep her distracted, I'll do the rest." I said ignoring Pollux.

"Yes, my lord." She left.

"What do I do?" Pollux asked anxiously.

"Stay out of the way." It was harsh but there wasn't really anything for him to do. "You can go terrorize people in the village if you want but don't do anything that will be in the national papers. Do you understand?"

He saluted me. "I'll only rob." He teleported away in a puff of smoke.

In all honesty I really didn't need Sofia either. I could've found Aquarius on my own but I had a plan. Correction, I had a genius plan. I found the throne room once again and Virgo and

Sagittarius were still playing music. Sagittarius stopped playing this time.

He set his flute down beside him. "You're plan will not work."

"You're a mind reader now?" I asked stepping in closer to him.

"I don't have to be." He stood up.

Virgo, still playing her harp, smiled. "We should have killed you."

"I can't die."

She stopped playing. "Let's test that theory shall we Sagittarius."

A bow and arrow appeared in his hand. "I remember what that dark force looked like. I remember the appearance well. The person dressed in black armor and wore a red cape. They sat on a golden throne and had a sword gem encrusted with a golden handle. They had it lying on their right thigh comfortably. A girl brought the person a golden crown that had Gems that strangely resembled our own. On the head of the person was tattooed CASTOR and the T looked like a cross."

I shook my head. The description was just like what Witch Greta showed me. It was official. I wiped my face. "Take your best shot."

Virgo stood and vines grew from the marble floor. Sagittarius aimed at my chest.

"Now!" I yelled. The arrow hit my heart and the vines stabbed at my chest and abdomen. I felt the blood leave my body. I looked and saw that my blood was black instead of red.

I stood up straight and pulled the vines and arrows from my body. I felt the black blood and shook my head. "So, gods bleed black blood?"

"You are no god." Virgo said quietly.

"Well then I'm immortal." The blood started drying up but you could see where the blood stained my clothes.

Sagittarius shook his head and turned to Virgo. "It's time."

She rolled her eyes. "Let's see if his plan works first."

I nodded. "It will."

"No, it won't." Aquarius entered in front of Gemini.

Gemini held Sofia by her arm and released her to me. "We are not ignorant of you. We knew your plan before it was even a thought in your head."

"What plan my lord?" Sofia asked.

"It doesn't matter now." I whispered so only she could hear me. "Where's Pollux?" I asked them.

Cancer levitated in the room. It was obvious that he didn't hear any of our conversation. "I see that you two found Sofia." He said to Aquarius and Gemini.

"Cancer, make yourself useful and go get the other Elders." Gemini ordered him.

"Why can't you do it?" He said placing himself on the ground.

"I'll do it." Aquarius said. He looked at me through the corner of his eye.

"I've already done it." Sagittarius said lying in his throne.

The other Zodians walked to their thrones and took a seat. About three seconds later the remaining Zodians, excluding Taurus, were sitting in their prospective seats. Libra was the last to arrive. He looked at the empty throne and then at Sagittarius.

Sofia shook her head and smiled. "You can't call a meeting without all of the Zodians."

"Shut up." Virgo said to her.

"Well she is right." Aries said.

"Call him." I whispered to Sofia as the Zodians murmured to each other.

She nodded. "Daddy!" She yelled without hesitation.

The murmurs stopped and everyone stared at her. She tried it again. "Daddy!"

Nothing. She sighed. "He should've come by now."

The Elders knew she was right. Something happened to him. It had to be something bad. Taurus was the type of father to come whenever his daughter called him, no matter what he was doing.

"Where could he be?" Sofia asked worried.

Cancer looked at me. He didn't say anything but I had a feeling that he was reading my mind. It was unnecessary for him to do that. I honestly had no idea where Taurus was. Maybe he was coming and Pollux stopped him.

Speaking of Pollux, he came crashing through the ceiling and landed in front of Sofia and I. At first, I stood there in shock. Pollux was lying in front of me bleeding at my feet.

"Pollux?" I knelt down beside him. He shouldn't have been bleeding actual blood if he was immortal.

"Look out!" Sofia pulled me back as her father landed on top of Pollux.

"No!" I yelled.

Taurus looked at me and then at the body under his feet. "What? He got in my way." He said with a smirk.

"Get off of him!" I kicked Taurus's stomach and was shocked at what happened next. Taurus didn't stay in the same spot. He flew into the thrones and nearly crushed Libra.

I looked at Pollux who was looking at me. "Nice shot bro."

"Help him." I commanded Sofia.

She didn't react.

"Sofia, that's an order. Help Pollux or…"

"You just kicked and knocked down my daddy." She said backing up from me.

I stopped to think.

Libra tightened his fists. "The Balance, it's being thrown off somehow. I cannot stop its constant movement. It's shifting rapidly."

Fire came from the gold floors and moved around like the sea. Rain started falling from the ceiling but the fire still remained. Vines grew from the walls and the Zodians jumped from their thrones as they levitated in the air. A hole opened in the floor and the undead slowly pulled themselves up from the hole. Aquarius's throne started bending into shapes, first a circle, then a square, and so on. Silhouettes flew around aimlessly as arrows shot at them, for everyone that was shot two more would come.

"What's happening?!" I asked Sofia through the chaos.

"It's time." She said slowly.

That's all she had to say. The Zodians themselves weren't causing these things, I was. The ground shook and grass sprouted up as animals leaped from the gaping hole. All of this was me. It was my destiny. You can't change destiny.

"Enough!" I said yelling louder than I had ever yelled before.

Slowly everything went away. The fire, silhouettes, animals, and undead went into the hole just before it closed up. The water stopped falling and vines withered away. The thrones returned to normal and fell to the ground as the arrows fell with them. The grass died and there was now an awkward silence. I sat down and Pollux laughed as he coughed up blood. "That was totally awesome. Do it again."

"The Balance has returned to its rightful state." Libra informed everyone.

I looked at my hands. "Virgo, you were wrong when you said I was no god."

"What are you talking about?" She asked clutching Aquarius's arm in fear.

I replied back to her and all the Zodiac gods, "I AM a god. I AM a god!"

The Journey Continues

THANK YOU FOR YOUR SUPPORT!

Keep Watch for
Zodiac Saga 3

ZodiacSaga.Com

www.ingramcontent.com/pod-product-compliance
Lightning Source LLC
Chambersburg PA
CBHW070258120726
47910CB00007B/2305